A BRIDE FOR
THE MAVERICK
MILLIONAIRE

A BRIDE FOR THE MAVERICK MILLIONAIRE

BY

MARION LENNOX

First published in Great Britain 2013
by Mills & Boon, an imprint of Harlequin (UK) Limited.
Large Print edition 2013
Harlequin (UK) Limited, Eton House,
18-24 Paradise Road, Richmond, Surrey TW9 1SR

© Marion Lennox 2013

ISBN: 978 0 263 23674 3

Harlequin (UK) policy is to use papers that are natural,
renewable and recyclable products and made from
wood grown in sustainable forests. The logging and
manufacturing process conform to the legal environmental
regulations of the country of origin.

Printed and bound in Great Britain
by CPI Antony Rowe, Chippenham, Wiltshire

To the awesome women
of Romance Writers of Australia.
This year we come of age—twenty-one
years of fabulous support, friendship and
professional growth. From the women who
were there at our inception to the women who
form our strength now, I give you my thanks.

CHAPTER ONE

FINN planned to have nothing to do with Rachel Cotton, but the elderly passengers on the *Kimberley Temptress* disagreed. They'd been giving him advice since Darwin.

'You ought to make a play for her. Make an impression. What's a cruise without a bit of shipboard romance?'

So, like it or not, he made an impression.

He knocked her grandmother overboard.

It wasn't exactly planned. The ship's tour guides, Esme and Jason, were assisting passengers to step down the short landing ramp to the rocky beach. Esme's job was to hold each passenger until Jason had them safely at the other end.

She didn't hold Dame Maud long enough, and Maud wobbled.

Finn stepped onto the ramp fast, but not fast

enough. Maud swayed and lurched—and hit Finn, who was trying to manoeuvre past Esme.

He couldn't grab her in time.

She was in her eighties. The water was deep, she was heading for the bottom and, from the rocks, Rachel Cotton screamed in terror, launching herself back across the ramp to dive in.

Finn was the owner of the entire *Temptress* cruise line, but he was here now as a passenger, undercover, to observe the crew. Rescuing passengers was not his call. Neither was stopping more passengers throwing themselves overboard. Nevertheless, he didn't have a choice.

He grabbed Rachel, sweeping her up into his arms.

'Stay back!'

'Put me down. Let me go!'

She was cute and small and blonde—and loud and lethal. She twisted and kicked…right where a guy didn't need to be kicked.

He swung around and shoved her into Jason's arms.

'Don't let her go,' he commanded, and dived overboard even as he said it.

* * *

Held by Jason, who was almost as strong as Finn, Rachel could only watch as her beloved Maud slid under the boat and out of sight.

'Maud!' She could make Jason drop her—martial arts training told her how—but sense was beginning to kick in.

'He'll get her,' Jason said.

He must. She had no choice but to depend on Finn Kinnard.

She'd met Finn the day the *Temptress* left Darwin.

'This is Finn Kinnard,' the purser had told her, determinedly making the ship's forty passengers mingle. 'Finn's a boat-builder from the US. Finn, this is Rachel Cotton, and she's a geologist. You two are the only young singles on board. Have fun.' She'd flashed a suggestive smile, her implication obvious.

'What sort of boats do you build?' Rachel had asked, intrigued despite the implication.

He obviously wasn't intrigued in return. 'Small wooden boats,' he'd said curtly, and then, grudgingly, 'What sort of geology?'

'Big rock geology,' she'd retorted, even more curtly, and he'd smiled. But he'd moved on fast.

She got it. He was expecting her to launch herself at him.

As if.

She was vaguely miffed, but not much. There was too much to do and see to be offended— but she couldn't help but stay aware of him. The man was tanned, tall and seriously ripped. He also exuded an air of confidence and authority which didn't quite fit with a lone traveller staying in the standard accommodation section of the boat.

'He's gorgeous,' Maud decreed the moment she'd set eyes on him. 'And a boat-builder… Ooh, I love a man who can handle a hammer. Rachel, love, if you weren't in mourning, I'd say go for it.'

Rachel had been forced to smile. Others skated round Rachel's grief, but Maud was upfront.

'A shipboard fling could do you good,' she'd decreed.

Rachel wasn't the least interested in any sort of 'fling', but she conceded Finn Kinnard was definitely gorgeous. And also…nice. He was solitary but not aloof, making light-hearted banter with the older passengers on the ship, offering help when needed.

She needed his help. Right now he was heading under the ship.

Where Maud was.

And crocodiles.

This was the tip of Northern Australia. This place was crawling with crocs.

She couldn't see. *She couldn't see.* Jason was holding her and wouldn't let go.

'He has her,' Jason said, but he didn't sound sure. 'I think… Yes!'

For suddenly they could see. Finn had her under her arms, hauling her out from under the hull, and up.

Maud broke the surface before him. She choked and coughed, then looked wildly round for her rescuer, who'd surfaced behind her.

And, typically Maud, she took a deep and dignified breath and made an extraordinary recovery.

'Thank you, young man,' she managed, with only one or two coughs in between. 'Oh, dear, I believe I've lost my hat. No, don't even think of diving for it. I believe my travel insurance will pay.'

There was a burst of relieved laughter. The Captain himself was reaching down, lifting her high as Finn propelled her up from below.

The deckhands were reaching for Finn. Laughter aside, the threat of crocodiles was real.

Even on deck, Maud held on to her dignity. She stood in her soaked skirt, her button-up blouse and her sensible walking shoes, and she patted her silvery bun to make sure all was present and correct.

And Rachel? Jason couldn't hold her. She was back over the ramp, reaching to hug this woman who'd become such a friend.

'Don't hug me, girl,' Maud retorted. 'You'll make yourself wet.'

As if that mattered. Rachel hugged her anyway.

'Dame Maud, I'm so sorry,' the Captain was saying. 'It should never have happened. The crew should have systems in place...'

'Don't you dare think about disciplining the crew,' Maud said. 'I should have been more careful but, even so, I haven't had so much excitement for years. Being saved by a young man like Mr Kinnard… Ooh, it's enough to make an old lady's heart flutter.' She cast Finn a smile that was pure mischief and then she smiled at Rachel in a way that had Rachel thinking *Uh oh*. Light-hearted banter about matchmaking was maybe about to get serious. 'Now, if you give me a moment to put a dry skirt on, let's get on shore and go find these paintings. I haven't come all this way for nothing.'

'You'll want a few moments to recover,' Rachel said and, amazingly, Maud's eyes twinkled.

'Do you need to recover, young man?' she demanded of Finn.

'Um…no,' Finn said, sounding disconcerted.

'I may not look quite as good as you, dripping wet,' Maud decreed, eyeing his shorts and clinging T-shirt—and the body beneath—with blatant approval. 'But I'm a fast dresser. A dry skirt and blouse and I'm done. Stop fussing, Rachel, love, and let's get on with our adventure.'

Maud had decreed she wasn't shaken, yet it was Rachel who was shaking. Because of Rachel, Finn decreed that Rachel was right, they did need a few minutes' time out. He'd changed his mind, he said. He did want to change his clothes and it took ages to button his shirt. Fifteen minutes, in fact. Maud looked pointedly at his very unbuttony T-shirt but she smiled and acquiesced, and Rachel threw him a look of gratitude as she ushered Maud below.

I want to be like Maud when I'm her age, Finn thought, as he waited for them back on the deck. Indomitable. Taking whatever life threw at you and finding humour everywhere.

He knew a lot about Dame Maud Thurston. She was the matriarch of Thurston Holdings, and Thurstons was one of the biggest mining companies in Australia. Her biography was in every Australian *Who's Who*, so finding out about her had been easy.

Not so her travelling companion.

Until two days before sailing, Rachel's berth had been booked by Maud's grandson, Hugo Thurston. Then there'd been a swap, which didn't fit with Finn's plans.

Finn had researched the passenger list with care before he'd started on this venture. He'd wanted no one here who'd recognise him.

Finn's ships took small groups of passengers to some of the most remote places in the world. The *Kimberley Temptress* should be one of his most successful, travelling from Darwin to Broome while it gave its passengers a guided tour of the magnificent Northern Australian coastline. It wasn't. There'd been complaints—nothing disastrous, but in an industry that depended on word of mouth to advertise, bookings were falling off.

Finn had always kept a low profile. He'd travelled this route when he'd first taken over the line, but that was years before. None of the crew knew him in person. Fineas J Sunderson had thus become Finn Kinnard, undercover boss. He was here as a passenger, to watch and to listen.

Not to watch the passengers.

But he hadn't been able to stop noticing Rachel, and the underwater drama had only intensified his noticing. Her terror had been palpable, her affection for the old lady obvious to all.

Her attitude had her as Dame Maud's granddaughter, and that was how Maud treated her, yet *Who's Who* said Maud only had the one grandchild—a grandson—and they looked nothing alike. Maud was a big-boned, booming matriarch, whereas Rachel was blonde and tiny. Maud's clothes were plain but quality, yet Rachel dressed in shorts and faded shirts, and she tied her wayward curls back with a simple ribbon.

Little, attractive and unsophisticated. A passenger.

Steer clear, he told himself. Leave the lady alone. Even if she didn't resemble every woman his father had ever messed with, any hint of a romantic connection would interfere with his job. Even if he wanted a romantic connection.

Which he didn't.

Finally they reappeared. Maud seemed as indomitable as ever, but Rachel was white-faced and shadowed.

Shadowed seemed the only way to describe her. Even haunted.

'Hey,' he said, smiling at them both. 'That was fast.'

'Not as fast as you, Mr Kinnard,' Maud said approvingly. She grinned as she surveyed yet another T-shirt. 'Well done on the buttoning. But we have extra problems. You don't have to worry about lipstick.'

'You're right,' he said, grinning. 'For this cruise only, I've given lipstick a miss.'

Maud chuckled but Rachel barely managed a smile. She'd been badly frightened, he thought, and then, with a moment's acuity, he thought, this was a woman who'd seen bad things happen. This was a woman who knew life could change in an instant, from wonderful to tragedy.

'I'm sorry I kicked you,' she managed. 'I was...terrified.'

'Maybe I deserved the kicking,' he told her. 'I didn't grab fast enough. But we didn't come close to disaster. There were many people able to rescue Maud. I was simply the nearest. And crocodiles tend to assess their prey before attacking. If you use the same fishing spot on a riverbank three nights in a row you may well get snatched, or if you stay in the water for a while. But for anything disastrous to happen to your grandmother, she'd have been very, very unlucky.'

'I know,' Rachel said, but she still sounded subdued.

'And Rachel's not my granddaughter,' Maud told him, casting a sharp glance at Rachel. 'She's my friend, and she's a bit fragile. She lost her baby a year ago, and this cruise is part of her recovery.'

Rachel's eyes widened with shock. She turned to Maud, her face even whiter than before, and opened her mouth to protest, but Maud shushed her.

'Mr Kinnard was heroic in rescuing me,' Maud said, quiet but firm. 'I don't want him thinking we haven't accepted his reassurance. He deserves to know why you look terrified.'

'I'm...' Rachel shook her head, as if trying to haul herself out of the nightmare she was so obviously in. 'I'm sorry. I didn't mean to look...'

'If you lost your baby, you can look any way you need to look,' Finn told her. 'It's me who's sorry, for your loss, and for the shock you had just now. But if you feel you can still go onshore...' He motioned to Jason, who was standing by the gangplank, six feet two of gangly youth, looking decidedly anxious. 'Esme and one of the deckhands have taken the main group on up the cliff. Jason's been left behind to see if we can catch them up.'

'There are paintings closer to the ship than the

ones the group's heading for,' Rachel said, surprisingly. 'It's a bit of a climb, but I know Maud's fit enough to cope.'

'Your hip...' Maud said.

'My hip's fine,' Rachel said, more definite now. She cast a cautious look at Finn. 'I had an accident a long time ago,' she confessed. 'I'm moving on. The paintings sound great. If we can persuade Jason to let us go...'

'The crew's here for the passengers' pleasure,' Finn said. 'I don't see why not. Let's go ask him.'

Jason did know the art Rachel was referring to. The main group of passengers was heading to a large, easily accessible cluster, but this smaller section was closer, a little less accessible but seemingly no less spectacular.

Finn was still wondering how Rachel knew about them.

'I guess we could go there,' Jason said dubiously, and he radioed Esme to get the all-clear. He then proceeded to enjoy himself, giving his little group a great guided tour and helping Maud as they made their way onshore.

Jason was a good guide, Finn thought. The

crew members on his ships were handpicked for knowledge and people skills. Jason spoke of the ancient peoples of this land with enthusiasm, and Finn thought this enthusiasm was what the cruise needed.

It had it. Why wasn't it working?

Why had Esme been distracted this morning? She'd been working by rote, not noticing Maud was unsteady when she'd let her go.

And why had they needed to land on rocks? The plan was to land the passengers on the soft sandy beach, which was much safer.

They'd had to change their plans because they'd missed the tide. Engine trouble. Again.

Delays were an increasing part of this tour's problem. There'd been too many instances of delays, where passengers couldn't walk on promised reefs because the ship missed the tide; where beaches became inaccessible.

He'd had the ship checked over and over, but the ongoing problems were all small and niggling. A fuel blockage. An electronic malfunction that needed checking in case it signalled something more serious. Little things that he couldn't put his finger on that, combined, were messing with passenger enjoyment and thus his profit.

That was why he was here. It was what he should be thinking about this morning—but instead he was walking beside a gorgeous young woman in one of the most beautiful places on the earth and he thought he'd worry about business this afternoon.

Rachel was walking with a slight limp, but she wouldn't let him help her. 'It's time I started standing on my own two feet,' she retorted, but she'd smiled as he'd offered to help and her smile was lovely.

'I can't believe I'm finally seeing this,' she breathed as they reached the far side of the beach and started the slow climb up the cliff face. Maud was unashamedly holding Jason's hand, chattering happily as they clambered, and Finn and Rachel were left to themselves.

I wouldn't mind if Rachel did need help, Finn thought. Holding this woman's hand would be no hardship.

Why was he so attracted?

Maud did indeed wear lipstick, but Rachel wore no make-up at all. She was in jeans she'd cut off to make frayed shorts, a baggy man's shirt, sensible walking sandals and a battered Akubra over her curls.

She looked almost a waif.

Small and vulnerable. Maybe that was what attracted him, he thought, but it was also sending out warning signals. This was the kind of woman his father preyed on. His mother had fitted the mould. His grandmother had also been little and cute in her time—and dependent and emotional and hysterical.

He wasn't going there. Ever.

'How did you know about these paintings?' he asked, trying hard not to offer to help again as she struggled over a patch of loose shale.

'I've known about this region all my life,' she told him. 'I've read everything there is to read. I've dreamed of visiting it for ever.'

'But this is your first visit?'

'Yes. Thanks to Maud, I've finally been able to come. But I've visited it so often in books I feel I know it already. Did you know fossils are extremely rare through the Kimberley Neoproterozoic? This place is so ancient we know only fragments about it, and the land holds and keeps its treasures. Like this artwork. Bird nest remnants over the top date the art to over seventeen thousand years old, yet here it is, not in some air-conditioned gallery but untouched, where it's lain for so long...' She broke off then, and a slight flush tinged her cheeks. 'Whoops. Sorry. My sister would say, "Here she goes again". I'm a bit...obsessed.'

'With rocks and art?'

'I'm a geologist. Rocks are what I love.'

But she'd loved more than rocks, he thought as he watched her struggle up the cliff. She'd lost a baby. Somewhere there must be a man.

Maud hadn't said she'd lost a partner.

She was Maud's friend. She had a sister.

He wanted to know more.

No. Little and pretty—and a passenger. *He could not be interested.* He was on the *Kimberley Temptress* for two more weeks. Close confines. He knew exactly what happened when people were stuck together in fantasy land. His father had taught him that, far too well.

It had been easy to sign up for this cruise as Finn Kinnard—because he *was* Finn Kinnard. His father was Charles J Sunderson, owner of the Sunderson Shipping Line. His mother was Mary Kinnard, little, pretty and vulnerable, and their attachment had lasted less than a week. Theirs had been a shipboard romance, resulting in an unwanted child.

He wasn't going there in a million years.

'I'm sorry I bored you,' Rachel said and he realised he'd been quiet for too long.

'You're not boring me. Tell me about the rocks.'

She raised her brows. 'Really?'

'Cross my heart, serious,' he told her. 'All my life I've been waiting to hear about these rocks.'

And, amazingly, she grinned back.

'Okay,' she told him. 'If we're seriously talking rocks…I believe this place is made from proterozoic sediments, dumped on an Archaean craton. The craton's surrounded by a paleao protezoic belt, which includes mafic and felsic intrusions and, of course, mignatites and granulites.'

'Of course,' he agreed faintly, and her smile widened.

'You can see that, too? Excellent. But, of course, you'll also be noticing the huge amount of deformation that's happened during emplacement. That process is complex, but I'm more than happy to tell you about it.'

'If I ask you out to dinner some time, will you give me the full rundown?' he asked, even more faintly.

She chuckled. 'I'm sure to.'

'Then that's one dinner date that's never going to happen.' He watched her chuckle, and suddenly there was no tension between them at all.

Her chuckle was wonderful, and it should have him thinking of her as every inch a woman—and of course it did—but right there, in that moment, overriding everything, this woman seemed a friend.

Which was a weird thing to think, Finn decided, as she started battling her way up the scree again. How had it happened, this sudden connection? This thought that here was someone he could relax with?

He didn't have to think of her as small and vulnerable. The stereotype was shattered. This wasn't a potential shipboard romance. This was a shipboard friend.

A gorgeous friend.

A friend with a gammy hip and a lost baby in her history.

More, there was something about the relief in her voice as she'd laughed over the lost dinner date that said she was even more wary of complications than he was.

Friend would do nicely.

'So why are you cruising on your own?' she asked over her shoulder.

'Why not?'

'It's expensive, for one thing,' she retorted. 'Not sharing a cabin…'

'I can afford it.'

'Can you? I can't. I'm here because Dame Maud's grandson fell in love with my sister, and wanted to stay with her rather than cruise with his grandmother.'

'Fickle,' he said, mock disapproving.

'Isn't it just,' she said, and he heard the chuckle return to her voice. 'Men are like that.'

But, behind the words…he heard something in her voice that wasn't a chuckle.

'Not all men,' he said, keeping it even, and she paused and glanced back at him.

'No,' she said. 'Hugo's not fickle. He and Amy will be very happy.'

He could definitely hear pain, he thought. Did he want to ask?

No. Don't probe. This was none of his business.

Jason and Maud were moving further ahead. Maud still had hold of Jason's hand and was asking question after question. Finn and Rachel were left in their own beautiful world.

They were now high above the Timor Sea. The massive cliffs of the mainland towered above them, and hundreds of tiny islands dotted the seas beyond. This place seemed as wild and untouched as anywhere on earth. With Jason and Maud disappearing round a rock face, there was nothing in sight except rocks and sea and the tough wild plants that fought for survival. The sun was on their faces and Finn paused and thought that this was a place to get things in perspective. To get things right.

Rachel had paused as well and was gazing round her with awe.

'The people who painted here seventeen thousand years ago,' she whispered. 'This is where they stood. What an absolute privilege to be here.'

He didn't reply. There was no need. They simply stood and soaked in the sun and the place and the moment.

The silence stretched on, each of them deeply content, but at the back of Finn's mind was a keen awareness of the woman beside him. How many women would stand like this, he wondered, in such silence? How many women that he knew?

Such a person must have learned the blessing of peace. The hard way?

'We should get on,' Rachel said at last, seemingly reluctant. 'Maud will think we've fallen down a cliff.'

'Not her. She's having a wonderful time with Jason.'

'She is, isn't she?' Rachel smiled with affection. 'But Maud has a wonderful time with anyone. Her husband died a few months ago. She was shattered—she still is—but she puts it aside and concentrates on now. If she meets great people she embraces them as friends. If they're not great, then she's interested and tries to figure what makes them tick.'

'Have you known her for long?'

She smiled at that. 'Crazy as it seems, only for three weeks. We travelled on the *Ghan* together, the inland train running from Adelaide to Darwin. We were…Maud-embraced. My sister met Maud's grandson and pow, that was it. My job at the university in Darwin doesn't start until next month, so I took Hugo's place on the ship. It's surely no hardship.'

But the word had caught him. *Pow.* Everything else in her explanation seemed reasonable, but *pow*?

'That was fast. Love at first sight…' He couldn't help the derisive note.

'You don't believe in it?'

'Not in a million years. So how about you? Are you looking for pow yourself?'

'No!' The fear was back, just like that, and it brought him up fast.

He could have bitten out his tongue. What a stupid thing to ask.

'Uh oh,' he said ruefully. 'I can't believe I asked that. With what I know of you…that was extraordinarily insensitive. I'm so sorry. It's none of my business.'

'Like your private life is none of my business,' she conceded and managed an apologetic smile. 'I had no right to ask what you believe in—or why you're travelling alone. Or even why you're not wearing lipstick.'

He grinned and the tension dissipated a little. 'I guess it's okay to be curious,' he told her, and by mutual accord they started climbing again. 'We're not part of this ship's demographic.'

'Yeah, the passenger list comprises three honeymoon couples and everyone else is over fifty. Which leaves us hanging loose.' The strain had disappeared and friendship again seemed possible. 'I need to warn you,' she said honestly, 'Maud is a born matchmaker and, frankly, she's scary. Now she thinks of you as a hero, I'm thinking she'll try very hard to get us together. Maybe you should start a mad, passionate affair with one of the Miss Taggerts, just to deflect her.'

As the Miss Taggerts were both in their seventies, he was able to chuckle. And, thankfully, so did she.

The awkward moment was past. Excellent.

He needed to tread warily, he thought. He did want this woman to be a friend.

But nothing else. Despite Maud's intentions, he surely wasn't in the market for a relationship, especially not in the hothouse atmosphere of a cruise ship. *He did not believe in pow.*

But he did want her to be a friend, he conceded—even if she was a passenger and little—and exceedingly cute.

They rounded the next rocky outcrop and saw Jason and Maud, high on the cliff face, with Maud waving wildly down at them.

'They're here,' she boomed, her elderly voice echoing out over the wilderness. 'The paintings are here and they're wonderful. This whole place is magic. Come up and join the spell.'

'That's my Maud,' Rachel said, grinning. 'There's magic wherever she goes.'

And ditto for Maud's Rachel, Finn thought, watching her wave back, but he didn't say so.

He climbed up the scree behind her, careful of her even though she wouldn't accept help. He watched her wince as she put strain on her obviously injured hip. He watched her greet Maud with laughter and then he saw her quiet awe as she looked at the paintings she'd waited a lifetime to see.

The art was extraordinary. Here was the depiction of life almost twenty thousand years before, stylized men and women who bore no resemblance to any identifiable race, animals that were long extinct, sketches that showed this vast rocky cliff had once looked out over grassy plains rather than a sea that must be junior in the scheme of time.

Finn had seen paintings like these the last time he'd done this cruise. Even so, his awe only deepened, and Rachel seemed almost unable to breathe.

She moved from painting to painting. She looked and looked, making no attempt to touch. Finn's tour guides were trained to protect these wonders and Finn knew if Rachel tried to touch, Jason would stop her, but there was no need to intercede.

Maud was treating the paintings with the same respect, but Finn could see that half the old lady's pleasure was seeing Rachel's reaction.

Maybe that went for all of them. Rachel's wonder was a wonder all by itself.

She examined everything. She saw the obvious paintings and then went looking for more.
She slid underneath a crevice and found paintings on the underside of the rocks. She slid in
further so she was in a shallow cave.

'These look like pictures of some sort of wombat,' she called. 'On the roof. Oh, my... Come
and see.'

'I'm not caving for wombats,' Maud retorted
and Jason elected to keep his uniform clean so
it was Finn who slid in after her.

She was looking in the half dark. Finn had a
flashlight app on his camera phone. He shone
it on the wombat-type animals and he watched
her amazement.

'They can't have painted these here,' she
breathed, soaking in the freshness of ochre-red
animals that looked as if they'd been painted
yesterday. 'This will have been the rock face.
The gradual deformation of the magma will
have pushed it sideways and under. Imagine
how much art's hidden, but how much has the
cliff movement preserved? These rocks are the

sentinels of this art. Silent keepers. It does my head in.'

He thought about it, or he tried to think about it. Artwork in geological terms. He looked again at the wombats—and then he looked at Rachel.

She was lying in the red dust, flat on her back, with the rock face art two feet above her head. She'd wriggled under the rocks, pushing dirt as she'd wriggled. Her blonde curls were now full of red dust, and there was a streak of red running from her forehead to her chin.

With the flashlight focused on the wombats, she was barely more than a silhouette, and a grubby one at that, and she wasn't looking at him. She was totally engrossed in what she was seeing.

Friends?

That was fast, he thought ruefully. He'd decided he could think of this woman as a friend rather than…well, as a woman.

He'd thought it for a whole twenty minutes, but now he was lying in the dust beside her, her bare arm was just touching his, and he felt…

Like he had no business feeling. Like his life was about to get complicated.

Really complicated.

He did not want complications.

But she turned to him, her face flushed with excitement, and heaven only knew the effort it cost him not to take her face in his hands and kiss her.

How would she react?

The same way he'd react, he thought, or the same way he *should* react. He'd seen her fear. She didn't want any sort of relationship and neither did he.

'I can die happy now,' she breathed, and that was enough to break the moment. To stop him thinking how much he really wanted to kiss her.

'We're not wedged that far under the rock,' he managed. 'I think if we try really hard we should be able to wriggle out. Maybe dying's not an option.'

'But you know what I mean.'

'No,' he said, and figured maybe he needed to take this further. There was something in Rachel's voice that told him this place had been an end point, an ambition held close when things were terrible. *If I can just hang on long enough to see the Kimberley art...*

So now she'd seen the art, and maybe she'd need to do more than hang on, he thought. Given what he'd heard in her voice—maybe he should make a push to help her.

'There's lots of things I still need to do before I die,' he told her, firm and sure. 'Maybe not as magnificent as this, but excellent for all that. For instance, I believe today's lunch on board is wild barramundi. Then we have Montgomery Reef to explore and the Mitchell River and the Horizontal Waterfalls. And, after that, when we get to Broome I've promised myself a camel ride. I've been there before but never had time to explore. And I hear there are dinosaur footprints in the Broome cliffs. How could I die before I see them?'

She hesitated in the half light before she spoke again, and he knew he was right to have been concerned. 'I just…' she whispered.

'You just thought you could stop now? Think again.' He couldn't help himself. He leaned forward in the close confines of their cave and he kissed her, a feather touch, a trace of a kiss that brushed her lips and that was all. It had to be all.

'Life is great,' he told her, firmly and surely.

'Ghastly things happen, but life's still great. You remember what's lost with regret, but you still look forward. There's always something.'

'You speak like you know…'

'I'm not a wise old man yet, Rachel,' he told her. 'But I do know life's good, and I do know that if I'd died yesterday I wouldn't be lying here with you, and I do know there's life after lunch as well. So shall we go find out?'

She gazed at him in the dim light and he gazed right back at her. She was so close. He could reach out and take her in his arms and kiss her as he wanted to kiss her—but he knew he couldn't.

It wasn't fair. It wasn't right, and what was more, it'd make her run.

He was not his father.

Lunch. Sense. He managed a grin.

'There's mango trifle as well as barramundi,' he said. 'Who could ask for more?'

'How do you know?'

'Spying's my splinter skill,' he told her, mock modest. 'I broke the code for the day's lunch menu at breakfast.'

Her smile returned. It was a smile he was starting to know and starting to like. A lot.

'Mango trifle?' she managed. 'Really?'

'You have my word.'

'I guess seventeen-thousand-year-old art fades into insignificance,' she said, casting another look at the wombats.

'Not quite,' he said and managed not to kiss her again. That was twice he'd contained himself in as many minutes. He should get a medal. 'But it's close. You want me to haul myself out first and tug you after?'

'I can manage on my own,' Rachel said. 'I haven't done it very well yet, but I will now. I must.'

They walked back to the ship as a foursome. Jason and Rachel traded knowledge about the area, and by the time they reached the beach Finn realised Jason was eagerly soaking in a knowledge that was greater than his own.

Jason was a great kid and he was humble enough to recognise Rachel's in-depth knowledge of this area. He'd done tour guide training for the Kimberleys, but Rachel's background knowledge was awesome.

We could employ her, Finn thought, shifting

back to owner mode. She'd be an awesome tour guide for his company.

He'd be her undercover boss.

Not going to happen.

Besides, she was still handicapped. By the time they reached the ship she was making a visible effort not to limp.

'Hold Rachel's hand as she crosses the ramp,' Maud ordered him. 'I don't want anyone else falling in the water.'

He held out his hand, but Rachel shook her head.

'Take it,' he growled and she glanced up at him and flushed—and took it. They all visibly relaxed.

He led her onto the ship and then turned to make sure Jason had Maud safe.

'I'm fine,' Maud said, stepping nimbly back on board. 'This morning was an aberration. Will you have lunch with us, Mr Kinnard?'

'Thank you, but no.'

'Why not?' She fixed him with a gimlet eye and he was eerily reminded of two great-aunts who'd bossed him mercilessly as a child. In Maud's presence, he felt about six again.

'I prefer my own company,' he said apologetically. A man did have to be sensible. 'I have books I need to read.'

'So does Rachel,' Maud snapped. 'And what good do books do her? Why do you prefer your own company? Are you married?'

It was an impudent question. Maud met his gaze with a look that said she knew very well she had no business asking, but what use was old age if she couldn't take a few liberties?

He could have snubbed her—but he'd kind of liked those old aunts.

'No,' he conceded.

'Are you gay?'

Rachel choked but he managed to keep a straight face.

'No again.'

'This isn't one of those "This-is-my-honey-moon-I've-been-dumped-but-I'm-coming-any-way" set-ups, is it?' she demanded and Rachel gasped.

'Maud! That's enough!'

'I'm just asking,' Maud said, innocent as butter. 'He's gorgeous. There has to be a reason why he's on his own.'

He sighed. He didn't want to tell her to mind her own business, but this was one fiery, intelligent lady and if he didn't tell her something she'd go on probing. Maybe she'd even guess the truth.

'You don't need to tell us anything,' Rachel said firmly. 'Maud, leave the man alone.'

'It's no secret,' he said, and managed a rueful grin. 'I might not be married but I'm not exactly a loner. I have three blissful weeks without two kids, and I'm making the most of them.' He glanced at Rachel and he saw the vulnerability in her eyes—and then he glanced at Maud and thought uh oh, maybe admitting to having kids was just going to lead to more questions.

So close the door on them, here and now.

'What I'm about to tell you is a bit like telling you I'm an alcoholic,' he said, softly but deadly serious, 'then saying please don't give me a drink. What I'm saying is that Connie and Richard are both the result of shipboard affairs. I like travelling but I don't always like the consequences. Rachel says you like to matchmake,

Dame Maud. Well, if I were you, I'd keep your Rachel far away from me. Grant me my peace, Dame Maud, and leave me alone with my books.'

CHAPTER TWO

WHY had he said that?

He watched both their faces change. He watched Dame Maud fight for the courage to ask more questions. He met her gaze levelly, coolly and he saw her decide that she wouldn't.

She was a brazen old lady but she was also lovely. She knew when boundaries couldn't be crossed.

'Granted,' she said at last, finally moving on. 'Very well. Thank you for the warning. Mr Kinnard. Thank you also for rescuing me this morning.'

'We're very grateful,' Rachel said, and she smiled. 'But wow, you didn't need to warn us off so dramatically. The matchmaking thing was dumb. Maud's flushed with the success of her grandson's engagement to my sister, but enough's enough. I'm not about to fall into your arms—or anyone else's for that matter. How embarrassing. Maud, you're the limit. Now if you'll excuse us… We'll see you at lunch, Mr Kinnard, but I give you my word, we'll leave you alone.'

So that was that. Excellent.

Or was it?

He headed for the shower and soaked for a long time, thinking about the morning, thinking about why he'd said what he'd said.

He'd just met a woman he thought was adorable. Rachel Cotton seemed a woman he'd really like to get to know.

But…was this the way his father had thought at the beginning of each and every one of his shipboard romances? He wouldn't mind betting it was.

Finn's grandfather had built a line of cruise ships that were world-renowned for their luxury and the fantastic places they went. The old man had been passionate about his ships and the experiences he gave his passengers.

Finn's father, however, had inherited little of his father's acumen but all of his love of luxury. He'd travelled the world, playing the wealthy ship owner, turning the heads of women he sailed with. They became his passion.

He'd selected innocents. He had a type. Little, cute, vulnerable women, sailing alone.

Finn was the first of his three known children, born to three different mothers and then totally rejected by their playboy father. Finn's mother had returned from her once-in-a-lifetime cruise, nineteen years old, pregnant and sure her life was ruined. She'd died five years later, leaving Finn to be raised by his grandparents. As he'd grown old enough to enquire, he'd found he had a half-sister and a half brother who hadn't even had the support he'd had.

Finn's father had left the remnants of the shipping line to Finn on the condition he change his name. Finn's first instinct had been to refuse. He hadn't needed his father for thirty years; why take his money now?

But then he found out more about his younger half-siblings. They were still just kids, and both were desperately unhappy. Richard was packing shelves in a supermarket, but aching to study. Connie was working on an assembly line in a textile factory, and already starting to suffer from arthritis in her hands.

When his father had died, Finn had been working as a boat-builder. Maybe that was why his father had chosen him. His sources must have told him of Finn's passion for boats—or maybe it was the fact that Finn's grandparents had never thought of asking for his father's assistance. It seemed the other women who'd borne him children had tried to get support and failed. But...

'He gave us you, so we can't hate him,' his grandfather had told him. 'But I'm darned if we'll take anything else from him.'

Finn didn't need his father, or his inheritance. The cruise line was in financial crisis. Split and sold off, it'd produce little.

But Connie and Richard haunted him. They had minimal education and no way forward without help.

A boat-builder couldn't help them.

So he'd taken a risk. He'd accepted his father's name, sold off the bigger ships and put what was left into a small line of intimate cruisers. He tailored his cruises to make them ecologically wonderful, exciting, fun. He took a wage but the remaining profits went into a family trust. He and Connie and Richard thus all inherited.

And somehow he'd found a life he loved. He'd

established a relationship with Connie and Richard. He'd even become attached to two kids who were still disbelieving of their new life.

But now... Something was wrong with the *Kimberley Temptress* and he was determined to find out what. It was a challenge he relished.

He did not need the complication of being attracted to Rachel Cotton.

So he'd lied to her?

Not exactly lied.

Lied, his conscience told him. He'd implied that Connie and Richard were his children.

His half-brother and sister now shared his father's massive house with him. Somehow over the last few years they'd established a loose sibling bond. It was true he was enjoying three weeks without Connie's questionable taste in music, but as for escaping from children... Connie was now twenty-five, and Richard was twenty-one.

They still seemed like kids to him. They'd come from damaged homes. There were still times when they were vulnerable; when he needed to look out for them.

But they weren't children, they weren't his

and he'd implied to Rachel and to Maud that they were.

The deception had been necessary, he told himself as he showered. With the connection he felt between himself and Rachel—with this weird, uncalled for attraction, and with Maud obviously set on making the most of it—he'd done what he must to protect both Rachel and himself.

'You could have done it without lying,' he told himself.

'I didn't lie,' he said out loud.

'That's semantics. You deceived them. They're not women to be deceived.'

And deceiving women was what his father had done, not him.

The conversation was futile, he told himself. What was done was done. Go back to avoiding them and move on. Remember why he was here.

For instance, they'd missed the tide today. They'd not been able to spend nearly as much time exploring the rock art as had been promised in the cruise itinerary. Passengers were awed by the art they had seen, and they wouldn't be happy with the shortened visit.

And Esme, the tour guide, had been distracted. She'd looked tired.

A minor mechanical glitch and a tired tour guide. These were tiny things but they were enough to cast a shadow on what should have been a flawless morning.

So focus on that, he told himself. That was what he was here for. Not wondering about the morality of deceiving a woman he couldn't have anything to do with.

'There are things he's not telling us.' Maud plonked herself on her luxurious bed and glared at Rachel. 'The man's an enigma.'

'The man's told us more than we had a right to ask or know,' Rachel retorted, flushing. 'Enigma or not, Maud, you overstepped the mark.'

'I know I did,' the old lady conceded, and sighed. 'He just seemed so perfect. He still seems perfect, but if he really has a taste for shipboard affairs… Though why tell us? It doesn't make sense. He's an honourable scoundrel?'

Rachel giggled. 'I kind of like the concept,' she confessed. 'So he's here to ravish some unsus-pecting maiden who isn't me. Who, then? There aren't a lot of maidens left.' She met Maud's twinkle and chuckled. 'How about you?'

'Well, I won't be adding more children to his nursery,' Maud retorted and chuckled her agreement. 'But there's more to Finn Kinnard than meets the eye, mark my words. Scoundrel, though... Maybe you do need to stay clear of him.'

'I can look after myself.'

'If you can't, then he'll have me to deal with,' Maud retorted. 'But he obviously has no intentions where you're concerned.'

'He kissed me in the cave,' Rachel said and coloured.

'*He what?*' Maud sat bolt upright, and Rachel could almost see her antennae rise and quiver. '*What did you say*?'

'You heard. He kissed me.'

And she'd done what she'd planned to do. She'd shocked the normally unshockable Maud, who stared at her, open-mouthed.

'What...what sort of kiss?' she managed at last.

Rachel chuckled, and pretended to consider, as if academically interested. 'Not very hard.

It was more a brush of lips than a proper kiss. Maybe he didn't like it.'

'Did you like it?' Maud demanded and Rachel forgot about being academic and coloured a bit more.

'I didn't mind it,' she conceded. 'But I'm not looking for more.'

'Well… Maybe it's just as well I told him about your loss,' Maud said, sounding dumbfounded. 'Maybe that's what's making him confess all. If so, it's just as well. With your history, there's no way you need a scoundrel.'

'Even an honourable scoundrel?' Rachel demanded and grinned. In truth, she was as confused as Maud, by the strangeness of her feelings towards Finn as much as anything else. Why had she reacted like she had? In the dark of the cave… She'd almost kissed him back, she conceded. She'd felt him wanting to kiss her again, she'd known such a kiss was within her reach, and a part of her had almost thought about encouraging him.

Quite a big part.

Whoa.

'It's time to move on,' she said, returning purposely to being brisk and efficient. 'Shower and lunch and then the ship's cruising to the next fabulous place. With so much fabulous around, Finn Kinnard fades into insignificance.'

'He's not insignificant,' Maud said darkly. 'He may be a lot of other things, but he's never that.'

There was another excursion after lunch, and then a great after-dinner movie. After such a day, Rachel expected to fall into bed and sleep until dawn.

Or hoped. Instead she did what she so often did. She woke in the small hours, with the nightmares right where they always were.

The fear of this morning had brought back a too-recent memory of the moment her life had changed for ever.

One lost baby.

How long did it take to get past grief?

If only she didn't think it was her fault. She'd fallen in love with Ramón—handsome, charming, the lead dancer in her sister's ballet company—and someone who lied and lied and lied. She remembered that last awful day. She'd met him after work. He'd been with friends and she'd looked doubtfully at the empty glasses on the table. But—'I've had one wine, baby, but I'm not over the limit. Of course I'm driving us home.'

After the crash his blood alcohol level showed him once again as the liar he'd been throughout their marriage, but the damage was done. She'd been seven months pregnant. A little girl.

Lost because she'd wanted to believe his lies.

And Ramón hardly cared.

'Women miscarry all the time. Get over it. My ankle, though…I won't be able to dance for months. Quit with the crying, woman, and start worrying about me.'

Get over it.

She almost had, she thought. Or as much as she ever would. The appalling blackness had lifted in the last few magic weeks, travelling through the Outback with her sister, Amy, and with Maud and Maud's gorgeous grandson. She'd watched Amy fall in love. She'd scattered her baby's ashes at Uluru, where her grandmother came from, and she'd felt at peace.

But it still didn't stop her waking at three in the morning, with her hands on her belly, aching with loss.

She lay in the dark and let the ache subside, as she knew it must. She thought of what she'd done over the last few weeks. She thought of Finn's words.

Ghastly things happen, but life's still great. You remember what's lost with regret, but you still look forward. There's always something.

There was…Finn?

He'd kissed her.

Ridiculous.

Ridiculous or not, she was thinking of it, and she found herself smiling in the dark. There was no pressure from Finn. He'd declared himself an honourable scoundrel and backed away. She could remember the kiss without any expectation that it'd lead anywhere else.

It was not a scoundrel sort of kiss.

But she needed to remember the scoundrel, she told herself firmly, and tossed in bed and wondered if she could get to sleep again. She knew she couldn't.

Her hip ached.

It always ached. Ignore it.

Something else was superimposing itself on her thoughts.

The *Kimberley Temptress* wasn't big enough for a swimming pool. What it had was a spa pool, set into the deck on the boat's highest level. With such a limited adult-only passenger list— and because it was only four feet deep—there was no need for supervision or time restrictions. The pool was filled during the day with passengers soaking aching joints after strenuous shore excursions, but at night it lay deserted, a gleaming oasis in the moonlight.

The night sky would be awesome up there, Rachel thought. And the sun-warmed water on her aching hip would be even more awesome.

She and Maud had separate cabins. She wouldn't disturb anyone if she slipped upstairs and counted stars.

So… Enough of the lying here wallowing in the past. She was in one of the most magical places in the world. Get out there and enjoy it.

Finn was far back in the shadows of the top deck. The deckchairs had been cleared to make room for passengers to gather for cocktails at sunset. At dawn they'd be set up again, but for now they made a deep shadowed recess of stacked wood.

Stacks could be manoeuvred, just slightly, so that a passenger could set up one chair behind, far into the shadows, and doze and watch what went on around the ship in the small hours.

He was on this ship incognito because he suspected his crew was drug-running. Simple as that. Said out loud, it sounded appalling. It was appalling. He didn't want to believe it but, the more he saw, the more he thought he was right.

Each time he'd taken this cruise before, the crew was flawless. The cruise was flawless. Since then there'd been a gradual attrition of staff. This crew, this cruise, was less than flawless.

During last night's delay the *Temptress* had veered slightly off course. He'd dozed at the wrong time but had woken just as a small dinghy pushed away from the side.

He wasn't very good at this spy stuff. A real spy would never have dozed, but he was figuring things out.

Indonesia was close. The *Temptress* never left Australian waters so was never searched by customs officials. Drug transfer would be all too easy.

By his boat and his crew. The thought made him feel ill.

He would not go to sleep tonight.

And then she came.

Rachel.

There was one light up here, for safety's sake, forward of the spa pool. He watched through the mass of folded deckchairs as she slipped off her bathrobe, revealing her swimming costume. He watched as she slid into the water, and he heard her murmur of pleasure as the warm water enfolded her.

She lay back on the padded cushions at the side and gazed up at the night sky and he glanced up, too, and saw the Milky Way as one never saw it on land, as one could only ever see it where there was no one, nothing for miles.

As they were now. No civilisation for a thousand miles. The ends of the earth.

He shouldn't be here. He shouldn't be watching. He was starting to feel as if he was invading her space, her privacy.

So stand up and say hi? He'd scare the daylights out of her.

'Who's there?'

He froze. What the...? He was tucked right in behind the stacked chairs. There was no way she could see him. Was there someone else coming up to join her?

He could see out through the gaps in the stacks of seats, but that was only because she was in a pool of light. Surely she couldn't see in. Not when he was so shadowed.

'Who is it?' She was suddenly nervous, gripping the edge and starting to pull herself out.

It must be him. She'd sensed his presence and he was frightening her. No...

'Rachel, it's Finn,' he called. Whatever illegal things were happening, nothing seemed to be taking place tonight. Hopefully, no one below deck could hear.

'F...Finn?' She was half in and half out of the water, peering into the shadows. 'What are you doing?'

'Meditating,' he said, making his voice firm, abandoning his hiding place, strolling out as if it were the most natural thing in the world that he'd been sitting behind a stack of deckchairs in the small hours.

If the people he was watching had this woman's intuition…

'How did you know I was there?' he asked, trying to make his voice casual.

'My grandma was Koori,' she said, still sounding nervous. 'She was sensitive at the best of times, and when she was older she lost her sight. She reckoned if she had to learn to make her way by sound, we should, too. She'd take us out to the park at night, turn off the torch and make us tell her what was happening. And then she'd tell us whether we were right. Your chair scraped a bit—and then I thought I heard you breathing.'

'That's creepy.'

'Not as creepy as you hiding behind deck-chairs,' she retorted, reaching for her bathrobe.

'Don't get out,' he told her quickly, but not moving any further forward. He desperately did not want to frighten this woman. 'I didn't mean to invade your privacy. I've had my quiet time now. I'll go.'

She slid down into the water again, neck deep, and watched him. She'd tied her hair up, knotting it on top so it wouldn't get wet. She looked… stunning. A nymph in the moonlight.

Her fear was fading. Speculation took its place. 'Meditating,' she said thoughtfully. 'Like in Zen?'

'Yoni Mudra,' he said promptly. Back in his boat-building days, he'd built a boat for one interesting lady. Maud-ish, but with kaftans and cowbells. The entire time he'd built, she'd tried to convert him to whatever it was she followed.

He still wasn't sure what it was, but he'd enjoyed it.

And, to his astonishment, Rachel knew it.

'I've heard of Yoni,' she said thoughtfully. 'That's where you block your ears, cover your eyes, pinch your nostril and press your lips together with whatever fingers are left. Breathing's optional.'

'When I'm deep in meditation, that's a worry,' he said, starting to smile. She really was one amazing woman. 'I can go ten minutes without remembering to breathe.'

She chuckled, but then she said, 'You're lying.'

'How can you doubt me?' he demanded, wounded. 'I prefer mantra meditation, but humming my Oms would wake the boat.'

She chuckled, but then her smile faded and she

looked at him directly. She was floating forward on the cushioned pads at the side, her chin resting on her arms. Her attention was all on him.

'So you were hiding behind the deckchairs—why?'

'There's a good one set up at the back. It's comfy.'

'It would have been comfier if you'd set it up in the front.'

'I might have scared any chance wanderers with my weird breathing.'

She thought about that. 'How many chance wanderers have been up here?'

'None,' he admitted.

'But you were expecting some?'

'I was right to expect,' he said. 'Here you come, wanting to gossip…'

'Right,' she said dryly. 'Go back to your Yonis. I won't bother you.'

'I'm done with Yoni. My chakras have been wakened and they can't go back to sleep. So…' He surveyed her with care. He had frightened her, he thought. He should leave, but he had the feeling that she'd no longer feel safe here. He'd spoiled her night.

She didn't believe him about the meditation. Why should she? It was a crazy story.

He couldn't tell her the truth, but maybe he could make it normal. He could make her relax and then leave.

Leave?

What he'd really like to do—*really* like to do—was move closer, maybe even slip into the spa.

Right. Strange guy, hiding in the shadows and then jumping into the spa… She'd be justified in screaming the ship down.

'You can't sleep?' he asked, and she shook her head.

'Nope.' Nothing forthcoming there.

'It's the best time,' he said easily, shoving his hands deep in his pockets and lounging back against the ship's railing. Giving her space. Acting as if this were midday rather than the small hours. 'When I was a kid I used to escape at night,' he told her. 'My grandparents went to bed at eight o'clock. By nine they were asleep and I'd climb the tree under my window and head off for a night's adventures.'

'You lived with your grandparents, too?'

'My mother died when I was five,' he said briefly. 'She had what my grandma called spongy lungs. Bronchiectasis. I can barely remember her.'

'Our parents dumped Amy and me with Grandma when we were toddlers,' she told him. 'They were tired of playing families. Thank heaven for grandmas.'

'I'd say that, too,' he said. 'Grandparents rock. As do dogs. Gran and Pop were too old to keep me company, so I got my first dog when I was six. Wolf even climbed the tree with me.'

'Wolf?'

He grinned at that. 'He was a bitser,' he admitted. 'Contrary to his name, he'd lick you to death before he'd bite, but he gave me courage. Kid roaming the night with Wolf...cool. I'd never have had the same street cred with a dog called Fluffy.'

'I called my dog Buster,' she said, smiling back at him. Finally relaxing. 'Maybe naming him Wolf would have been better—but I suspect people would have laughed. It's too late now.'

'You only had the one?'

'I only *have* the one. Buster's staying with Amy during this cruise.'

'How old is he?' he asked, startled.

'Ancient. I didn't get him until I reached my teens and I've had him ever since. And yes, he's been my only one. When Grandma was alive we lived in apartments, no dogs allowed. When I found Buster we were with foster parents, and Amy and I had a heck of a job to persuade them to let us keep him.'

Foster parents…

Uh oh. The word made Finn take a mental step back. Warning bells were ringing. Petite and vulnerable…

But maybe vulnerable wasn't the right word.

'But, despite no Wolf, we learned martial arts,' she continued, reflective now, looking back. 'Amy and I are both black belt. That's served the same purpose as your Wolf, I reckon. You needed Wolf for protection, but we're fine with Buster. Amy and I can take on guys twice our size and win.'

'That would explain the kick,' he said faintly.

'I guess it would.' She eyed him with speculative enjoyment. 'If I'd really needed to get free…

We can throw men bigger than us. Do you want a demonstration?'

'No!'

'Pussycat.'

'I'm only a he-man when I have Wolf,' he admitted, growing more and more fascinated. The thought of Rachel climbing out of the pool and trying to throw him...

He could let her try.

Dripping wet woman. Body contact. Darkness.

Not a good idea, no matter how tempting— but heaven only knew the effort it cost to refuse.

She was still watching him with eyes that saw too much. He had to say something. Something that didn't evoke the image of Rachel in her swimming costume, trying to throw him...

'Wolf...Wolf died when I was fifteen,' he managed, moving right on. Or trying to move on. 'After Wolf came Fang—he was a Labrador who could leap tall buildings if a sausage was at stake. Now Connie has a cat called Flea.'

'Flea,' she said faintly. 'That's a horrible name.'

'The fleas were horrible, too,' he admitted, settling a little. Starting to enjoy himself. Starting to enjoy her. 'He was a stray who came with attachments. But we've conquered Flea's fleas.'

'I'm glad.' She gave a decisive nod, tucked her chin further down onto her folded arms, then proceeded to survey him with concentration. Her concentration was unsettling. He was developing an unnerving feeling that he wasn't able to hide from what she was seeing.

How much had her Koori grandma taught her? How to see past a man's defences? How to read lies?

Like who were these kids he talked of?

Don't ask, he pleaded silently, wishing suddenly that he hadn't mentioned Flea, a cat who led to his siblings.

'The kids…' she said.

He'd asked for this. 'Yes?'

But his tone must have instinctively said *Don't go there*, and she got it. She looked at him for a long moment and said, 'You don't want to talk about them?'

'I don't.'

When had that ever stopped a woman asking more? he thought. But, to his surprise, she nodded and obliged. With only the one sideways question.

'You'll go home to them when this cruise finishes?'

'I will.' He could answer that without lying.

Implying they were his had been stupid, he conceded, but his reasons for the defence they gave him still stood. And explaining now was unnecessary.

She had no need to know, and she'd moved on. 'Fair enough,' she said, and turned her attention upward. 'Do you know the southern sky?'

That unsettled him again.

This woman was a geologist. She knew the forms of meditation. She knew stars as well?

'Am I about to learn?' he asked dubiously.

She chuckled. 'This is no dinner date,' she assured him. 'So no lectures. And actually I'm not all that honed up on the constellations. The Southern Cross is pretty cool, though, isn't it?'

'It is.' It was. He'd been staring out into the darkness for the last few hours. The Milky Way was spread across the vast night sky and from here he could pick out thousands of individual stars; dot points of light that combined were a mass to take a man's breath away.

As was the woman smiling up at him.

The desire to slide into the pool with her was almost overwhelming.

He was fully clothed. He was sensible.

A sensible man should leave.

He couldn't. He physically couldn't.

Maybe he could compromise. He slipped off his shoes, rolled up his trousers and slid down to sit on the edge. Not so close to be intimate. Close enough to be companionable.

She looked up at him and she raised an eyebrow. 'Not coming all the way in?'

'Your Maud should take better care of you,' he growled. 'I warned you. What are you doing, cavorting in spa pools…?'

'With honourable scoundrels…'

'Pardon?'

'That's what Maud and I have decided you are,' she said blithely. 'We're not sure whether we believe you or not, but we're giving you the benefit of the doubt.'

To say he was disconcerted would be too light a description.

Producing Richard and Connie to divert Maud's matchmaking plans had been a spur of the moment decision, made almost light-heartedly. Rachel's description of him as an 'honourable scoundrel' was similarly light-hearted, but there was a major part of him that was saying he didn't want to be categorised by this woman.

He'd done it to himself.

'Do you play Scrabble?' she asked, which disconcerted him all over again.

'Scrabble?' he managed blankly, and she stared up at him as if he'd arrived from another planet.

'You haven't heard of Scrabble in the US?'

'I…yes.' His grandparents used to play. A lot.

'Well, here's an invitation no playboy can resist. Every day after lunch, when everyone else is supposed to be taking a nap and recuperating for our next adventure, Maud and I play Scrabble in the rear lounge. If you feel like a challenge, you're very welcome. Mind, we take no American spellings—and we take no prisoners.'

Scrabble…

With Maud.

And Rachel.

He thought back to this morning, to his idea

that this woman could be a friend. Here she was, offering friendship.

She was lying in the spa bath in the moonlight looking so lovely she took his breath away.

She was smiling at him quizzically, and he thought of her black belt in martial arts. He'd produced Connie and Richard to protect her as much as to protect himself—and suddenly he knew this lady needed no such protection.

She wasn't interested; it was as plain as that.

She was offering him friendship.

And suddenly, irrationally, he was looking at her and wanting more.

No. He was here as a loner, an undercover boss, here to find out what was messing with his business. He had neither the time nor the inclination for any relationship.

Except Rachel was here and he definitely had an inclination for a relationship.

It couldn't happen. Not here. Not now. Maybe later, when they were safely on shore, he thought, when Rachel was on her own ground, when he'd cleared up this mess and was able to tell her the truth.

Meanwhile…Scrabble or nothing.

'Done,' he said weakly.

'We're good,' she warned him.

'So am I.'

She eyed him speculatively in the dim light. It was the weirdest feeling. This was a romance setting to end all romance settings. Moonlight on the top deck of a luxury cruise ship. Calm waters, a warm, gentle breeze, the moonlight a ribbon of silver across the water. A heroine in the spa pool, lazing back in her swimming costume, her hero beside her, not in the water but close enough to touch.

This was doing his head in.

'I'm used to winning,' he managed and she grinned.

'Excellent. I do love to see a man brought down to his proper place in the scheme of things. I should get out now and go back to bed. I've no intention of playing to-the-death Scrabble on too little sleep.'

She twisted in the water and tugged herself out. He rose, and saw her falter as her gammy hip gave a little.

Instinctively he rose, reached and held her, settled her, made her safe.

She was dripping wet, beautiful…and so close.

'We prefer passengers to keep off the decks after midnight.'

He turned and saw Esme, the senior tour guide, staring at them from the top of the stairs. She was carrying a powerful torch which shone straight at them, and her expression wasn't friendly.

Rachel tugged backwards, but the edge of the pool was too close. Her hip wasn't working, and he wasn't letting her go. Esme was making them feel like two kids caught behind the shelter sheds.

His arm came around Rachel and held, and he met Esme's gaze full on.

'Take the beam from our faces,' he said harshly, and she shone it for just a moment too long before she did.

Time enough to make him angry.

This was a private cruise. It was billed as luxury, and it was advertised as a cruise where you had the freedom of the boat. The bridge was open at all times. Passengers were free to go in and chat to the captain or the crew. They could ask to be taken down to the engine rooms if they wanted—they needed escorting, but that rule was simply for passenger safety. The whole ship was available, wherever and whenever the passengers wanted.

And here was Esme, saying it wasn't.

'Why shouldn't we be up here?' Finn asked, pleasant but firm, still holding Rachel.

'It's not safe. If something happened...'

'The sea's calm. The night's lovely. You have high, safe railings. What's the problem?'

'We prefer...'

'The literature says we're free to use these decks at any time.'

'And if something happens?'

This was the reason he was here, Finn thought grimly. This woman's attitude was messing with his cruise line. Esme's qualifications were superb but right now she was acting like a schoolteacher, and a crabby one at that.

'I'm going back to bed,' Rachel said, and finally tugged away.

'Rachel, you have the right to be on any deck at any time you choose,' Finn said in a voice that brooked no argument. 'Unless the Captain has put up a bad weather warning, we're free to be here. Isn't that right, Esme?'

'It's what's in our guidelines,' she admitted grudgingly. 'But we expect you to be sensible. The upper lounge is comfortable and has enough places to be private.' She looked from one to the other and her look was almost offensive. 'If you need privacy…'

She has to go, Finn thought. No matter her qualifications, she was not who he wanted on his ship.

But he couldn't sack her now, and Rachel was already retreating.

'I'm off to bed anyway,' she said. 'Goodnight.'

She left. He wanted to hit something.

Turning his mind back to his suspicions, and wondering.

Maybe Esme was simply a grumpy crew member, rostered on for security as most crew members were, and wanting to make life easy for herself.

Or maybe she had ulterior motives for keeping the decks clear.

'I'm sorry I interrupted you,' she said grudgingly. 'But you really would be more comfortable inside.'

'In my own good time.'

'Sir…'

'I know what I paid for.'

'Well,' she said, 'at least Miss Cotton has seen sense. Don't fall overboard.'

'I'll try my best,' he said and watched her retreat in a huff. He thought about what was happening on his ship—and he also thought how good it had felt to hold Rachel Cotton.

Sensible or not, he knew which thought was taking precedence.

CHAPTER THREE

THE next morning they landed in the cove where *HMS Mermaid* had foundered over a hundred years ago. The Cutter had been nail-sick—leaking badly. The nails had rusted out and every nail had to be removed and replaced before the ship could safely sail on. During their enforced stay the crew had carved the ship's name and date on one of the distinctive native boab trees that must have been large then, but was vast now.

The cove was beautiful, the weird bottle-shaped Australian boabs were spectacular—and Finn couldn't get close to Rachel.

She was surrounded by elderly ladies. She'd greeted him easily at breakfast, but otherwise he was just another passenger and she had friends all around her.

Not including him.

After they'd seen their fill of boabs, the passengers split. Jason was leading a strenuous cliff climb, and Esme was leading a gentler cliff walk.

Jason assumed Finn would be on his team, and seeing Rachel join the cluster of little old ladies around Esme, Finn thought joining them would be too obvious.

Why was Rachel with the old ladies? Was it because her hip hurt or because she was avoiding him?

That was his ego talking, he told himself, and it didn't matter. It was good, in fact. He wasn't interested.

But he glanced behind as Jason led the way up the track—and caught Rachel doing the same.

Their gazes met—and then Rachel deliberately looked away.

Liar. He was interested.

At lunch Finn sat with a honeymoon couple and a farming couple from Queensland. The farmer and his wife were great company. The honeymoon couple were playing footsies under the table.

Finn was trying to be good company, but he

couldn't stop being...interested...in a slip of a girl two tables away.

The average age of Rachel's table must be ninety, yet she didn't seem to notice the age disparity. Her table erupted in laughter over and over, and he thought, here's a woman coping with tragedy but there's no way she's letting it interfere with the happiness of those around her.

How much of the bubble of laughter was an act?

He didn't know.

He shouldn't be interested.

After lunch, as instructed, he headed for the deck where Scrabble was promised.

If his mates at the boat-building yard could see him now...

He grinned, and then he thought of one of his fellow apprentices. Sean had been spotted through the window of his girlfriend's house, and she'd been using his hands to help her spool wool. Pink wool.

Sean had been given heaps, but he hadn't minded nearly as much as Finn thought he would.

'I'm keeping her happy,' he'd said serenely. 'She's worth any amount of pink wool. She's a good 'un.'

Was that where Finn was now? Doing what it took to make a woman happy?

No. Friends. Not interested.

He pushed open the lounge door and stopped short.

'Come in.' Rachel beamed a welcome. 'We're ready. Isn't it lovely; we've found more players. The Miss Taggerts play, too. We've decided five's too many for a satisfactory game so we've split. I'm playing Maud and Miss Veronica, and you're playing Miss Margaret.'

'Call me Margaret,' his elderly opponent said, beaming her pleasure at having Finn all to herself. 'Next you can play Veronica. If we're fast you can get round all four of us.'

He played two excellent games of Scrabble, one with each of the Miss Taggerts. They played well, and he almost found himself enjoying it—except he wasn't playing Rachel.

She was watching him, approving, he thought,

as he concentrated fiercely on not being beaten. But approval suddenly wasn't enough.

Was he nuts? What had changed? Why was this woman becoming so important to him?

He'd made a vow about fellow passengers.

He was close to making a vow about women in general.

So much for vows. Her laughter had him intrigued, wanting more.

'Another match tomorrow?' Maud demanded as they finished the second game and the intercom announced the next expedition.

'Fine,' he said weakly.

'Rachel's booked a radio phone call to her sister tomorrow,' Maud said. 'So that leaves just the four of us. What say we play two against two?'

And Rachel's lips quirked—and he saw laughter and mischief in her lovely brown eyes

'You're doing okay,' she said softly as she passed him on the way out. 'For a scoundrel.'

Two more days. Shore excursions, laughter, Scrabble—nothing more.

Finn was starting to go nuts.

Waiting was hard.

He was waiting for the crew to slip up, waiting to see if he could prove his suspicions. But he was also waiting for the cruise to end—so he could decide whether he could think about maybe…

Maybe going somewhere he'd never gone before?

Unknown territory. Uncharted waters.

And then the ship stopped.

He wasn't asleep this time. Finn wasn't a guy who needed lots of sleep and he had enough on his mind to keep him awake into the small hours. He'd been tracking the ship's course on GPS, comparing it to the maps he'd packed. He knew, therefore, that the *Temptress* was off course and he wanted to know why.

As the engines slowed, he slipped out into the night. Not to the top deck. Rear mid deck, he thought. If his suspicions were correct… If there was anything to be transferred it'd be easiest from the lowest level, and the mid deck overlooked the lower.

He was wearing dark chinos and a black T-shirt. He should blacken his face, he thought ruefully—but then, a passenger wandering the decks at night was normal. A passenger with a blackened face? Not so much.

But nobody saw him. It was easy to slip through the darkened passenger quarters, easy to find himself a shadowed nook overlooking the rear, easy to settle with his phone camera—and wait and see what his crew was using his ship to do.

The ship had stopped.

Had they reached their destination? The crew usually used the passengers' need for sleep to transport them from one wonderful spot to another. Rachel had looked at the map last night and thought they'd be travelling all night.

They must have made good time if they were there already.

The wind was getting up a little and the sea was choppy. She lay in her luxurious bunk—okay, bed—and wondered where they were.

She wondered all sorts of things. She'd been wondering for hours.

Sleep was a luxury that had been destroyed

the night her baby had died. She slept in patches now, in between dreams.

If she was at home she'd get up and watch something inane on the telly. Anything was better than lying here and thinking of her baby—and thinking of Finn Kinnard.

She wouldn't mind another spa, she thought, but Esme had taken her aside and given her a solid talking-to. 'Please don't go out onto the decks after midnight. The ship rolls. Even though it looks stable, the top deck gets quite a list when the sea's choppy. I know the spa's lovely but we wouldn't want you or Mr Kinnard to be lost overboard.'

But Finn had said—solidly—that they had the right to be there. The decks were well railed and she was sensible.

She really wanted to see where they were—and she'd had enough of staring at nothing.

She wouldn't go near the top deck again, she conceded. Spas in the moonlight… Okay, been there, done that. Finn could have them on his own. But if she went to the rear lower deck she could watch the moonlight on the water. Get some perspective.

Think about...nothing?

She wouldn't think about Finn Kinnard. She'd think about *nothing*.

And no swimming costume this time.

She wasn't planning to stay out there. She had no intention of running into Finn again. Not in the dark. No way. She'd slip out and take a look and then retreat.

She'd only be out for a moment... Just for a look... There was no chance she'd bump into Finn again. She wouldn't even have to get changed.

Decision made, she tugged on a jacket over her nightdress and headed for the deck.

There was no way the ship should be here.

Deviating from the prescribed route was itself a cause for huge concern, Finn thought grimly. These waters were littered with uncharted rocky outcrops. The route for the *Kimberley Temptress* was carefully planned to avoid them; to ensure there was no risk to the passengers, who were Finn's sole responsibility.

But his GPS told him they were miles north

of their chosen route, and the ship seemed to be drifting.

Why were they here?

The ship was almost in darkness and that was another cause for concern. There should be lights along the rails. The bridge was still lit, but faintly, and the back of the deck was in darkness.

Finn edged to the rail, staying in shadows. People were moving below him on the aft deck. Shadowy figures. Two? Three?

They were at the rail, looking out to sea.

And then, so quietly that if he hadn't been straining to hear, he could have missed it, came the sound of oars. An expert rower, moving fast but with stealth. There was barely a splash.

The people below him opened the guard rails, allowing access to the open sea. The rowing boat was right there, tossing a rope to be caught, tugged to lie alongside. Flashlights flicked on. One of the crew...Esme, he thought, recognising her slight figure...knelt and received something from someone in the boat, handing it back to those waiting behind her.

'We should have got it all last time,' Esme

hissed furiously, as Finn strained to hear. 'Next run, one drop. No matter what we pay, the Captain's getting edgy.'

'The weather was too clear and there was a yacht too close for safety.'

'It's our call whether it's safe or not.'

'We're not putting our necks on the line.'

'If you're going to be a coward...'

But whoever was in the rowing boat didn't like having his courage slighted. There was an oath, and the next package was hurled rather than passed. Esme tried to catch it and missed.

The package hit the deck with a thump, revealing silver paper, ripping as it landed. Finn caught a glimpse of something white spilling out.

'Have you guys caught something? Can I see?'

And, from where he stood, Finn recognised Rachel's voice and froze. No!

Bad had suddenly become a whole lot worse.

Esme whirled and her flashlight lit the newcomer. Its beam hit Rachel—who was looking absurdly cute in nightdress and jacket, but she also looked confused.

She must have come down the outside steps to see what was happening, Finn thought. She'd think this was a bit of night-time fishing. The silver package would have looked like a fish thumping on the deck. A couple of the old guys on board fished here during the day.

Normal.

Bu there was nothing normal about this. The beam from Esme's flashlight hit her in the face and she flinched.

One of the men flicked his flashlight at the split package.

It definitely wasn't a fish.

'Turn that off,' Esme snapped, but it was too late. Rachel would have seen—as Finn had seen—the parcel, its white powder spilling onto the deck.

And Rachel's face changed.

'I'm sorry. I…I'm intruding. I'll go back to bed,' she managed and stepped backward but Esme moved faster, gripping her arm with a force that wrenched her forward.

'Let me go.'

'Don't hurt her, boss,' the engineer said, sounding appalled. 'She's a passenger.'

'She's seen.' Esme's voice was a vicious hiss. 'Hell. We have no choice. I won't let this mess us up.' *This.* She was speaking as if Rachel was a thing rather than a person. A thing that had got in the way. 'She goes overboard—now.'

Another man was behind her, shoving her closer to the rail.

Three against one. Martial arts training was never going to help Rachel here. They were pushing her, hard.

Bad had turned to appalling. Bad had turned to *do something now*!

The smart thing would be to go for help—smart for him, but not for Rachel. He could raise the ship but it'd take minutes and meanwhile Rachel was being dragged inexorably to the open gate.

He had seconds. There was no choice.

'Leave her be.' He stepped out of the shadows, yelling, his voice booming across the stillness of the night. 'Let her go, now!' He headed down the stairs three at a time, out onto the deck—where three of his crew were suddenly holding guns.

He hadn't anticipated guns.

He hadn't anticipated anything.

Wrong. He'd guessed drug running could ex-

plain the constant delays. He just hadn't anticipated it could be so…deadly.

The thought of his crew drug running made
him feel ill—but what was making him feel
worse was the sight of two guns aimed straight
at him, and one aimed at Rachel. And Rachel
was already far too close to the open gate.

'Get with her,' Esme snapped at him and
shoved Rachel further toward the gate. She
stepped back. Rachel managed to grab the side
rail but only just. Esme motioned the gun at
Finn. 'Now. And one more word out of you and
I'll shoot.'

Guns were pointing straight at him. Leaving
was not an option. Neither was shouting.

Somebody might already have heard.

Nobody was coming.

'You can't shoot them.' The engineer sounded
and looked appalled. 'Hell, Es, we'll have the
country on our heads.'

'There's rough weather ahead,' Esme snarled.
'If they fall in some time before dawn, what fault
is it of ours? These two have already been re-
ported as carousing on the top deck. We'll toss
a couple of champagne bottles around, make

it look like it was a party. The crocs will get them—but we'll make sure first.'

And, with no hesitation at all, she raised her gun and she aimed at Rachel.

And Finn dived straight at Rachel, and knocked her overboard.

She could swim, and she didn't panic.

He learned that about her in the first seconds after they hit the water. He grabbed her hand as they fell, and held. Instead of flailing for the surface, she twisted toward him underwater and he felt her make the decision to stay with him. He tugged her down, and she came, diving back beneath the ship and sideways.

They had to release hands to fight their way under the shelter of the hull, but he kept with her, just touching. Holding his breath as long as she did. Each moved instinctively away from the murderous thugs at the ship's rear.

Thank God the boat had stopped. Thank God there were no propellers.

They surfaced towards the front of the ship, as close to the hull as they could get. They were shocked to numbness, but tucked right under the forward hull was the safest place for them. They couldn't be seen unless someone walked along the rail, bending over with a flashlight. Searching. With a gun.

Maybe someone would.

'I can scream,' Rachel whispered, sounding stunningly composed. 'My scream can wake the dead.'

He thought fast, and rejected it just as fast. 'You heard them,' he managed. 'Even if someone's already heard yelling… It'll play to their story. We fell, they saw us, they saw a croc. Once they know we're here, they'll have no choice but to shoot.'

'Then…' Her composure faltered.

'We need to swim,' he whispered, his thoughts bleak as death but knowing it was their only chance. 'They can't search. If they put on floodlights they'll wake the boat. Unless they're sure they can kill us before anyone else reaches the deck, they can't risk it. The water's choppy. They won't be able to see without searchlights. How well can you swim?'

'As far as I must,' she said, calm again, and if

he was astounded already at her composure, he just grew more so.

But he didn't have time to be astounded. There was only time for survival.

'The tide's going out. The current will take us north.' He was thinking as he was whispering, holding her with one hand, touching the hull with the other to make sure they didn't drift out from the ship to where they could be seen. 'There's an outcrop a few hundred yards to our north. That's obvious—if they send out a tender to search they'll find us—but there are smaller outcrops behind. Do you think…?'

'Give me a minute.'

'We don't have…'

But she was fast. She was twisting herself out of her jacket, whirling it into a rope, knotting it round her waist. 'Just making me streamlined,' she explained. 'Go.'

They went.

It was the swim of nightmares, but the night-mares had to be blocked out or tempered with reason.

The water was rough and ink-black, and behind them were people who wanted them dead. The guy in the rowing boat played in his mind. He'd have come from a bigger boat. If the *Temptress* left the area, he could use searchlights.

But the guy was angry with Esme, he thought. That might help. He wasn't a crew member. He'd know neither Finn nor Rachel would be able to identify him—or the boat he came from. He may well refuse to search for someone who couldn't necessarily incriminate him.

He decided to hold that thought and block out others.

Like reef sharks. Like crocodiles.

They were in the open sea. Crocs usually stayed close to land, sticking near estuaries and river mouths.

They did go further afield…

And reef sharks? Don't go there, he told himself. It achieved nothing to know that any minute they might be a sea creature's snack.

They. That was the word to keep nightmares at bay. Beside him was Rachel, swimming strongly and steadily alongside him.

He needed to rein back to keep beside her but that was no hardship. They swam so that at every second stroke their hands touched. They swam as if they were rowing, stroke for stroke, keeping solid, steady rhythm. Together.

The feeling grew, a solid, tangible comfort. Apart, there was nothing but the sea and the blackness and the fear, but together they could do this.

He was aware of her as he'd never been aware of a woman in his life.

They couldn't stop except for occasional gasping pauses where he tugged her hand and stilled and checked the horizon until he found what he was looking for—a rocky crag lit faintly by the moonlight. Each time he signalled to her, adjusted their course, pressed her hand—that part seemed more and more important—and then kept right on going.

There was no room and no energy for talk. There was nothing but the sea and the blackness and each other.

This was no short swim. An hour? Who knew? Time couldn't be measured. He wasn't trying to measure. There was a crazy intimacy within this peril and, weirdly, he found himself thinking of the sensation.

He didn't do intimacy.

Finn was the only child of a sickly, emotional woman whose life had been shattered by her loss of control. His grandmother had been even more emotional, disintegrating when her daughter died and never recovering. By the time she, too, had died, when Finn was fifteen, he and his grandfather had suffered enough emotion to last a lifetime. 'You keep your feelings to yourself,' the old man had told him, over and over. 'You don't inflict them on everyone else. It gets you nowhere.'

And when he'd questioned the old man's stony face at his grandmother's funeral, his grandfather had turned on him.

'You don't need people,' he'd snapped. 'Look at your grandmother. Your mother died and she decided her life was over. She did nothing but weep for ten years until she died herself. That sort of emotion…it destroys people and you're better without it.' He'd stared down at his wife's fresh grave and his face had grown grim. 'Ten years of grief, followed by yet more grief,' he'd muttered. 'Learn from me, boy. You don't need people.'

That was how he'd been raised. Right now, though, Finn needed Rachel.

She wasn't as strong a swimmer as he was. Without her, he'd be closer to the island by now, but without her he'd also be alone in this appalling blackness—and alone was the way of madness.

Though…without Rachel, he wouldn't be here. Without Rachel, he could have stayed in the shadows, learned what he needed to learn to place this whole mess in the hands of the police when they reached Broome. It was Rachel stepping innocently onto the aft deck who'd thrown them into such deadly peril.

But then… It wasn't Rachel's fault.

The dark and fear were making his thoughts convoluted, twisting backwards and forwards.

Rachel was a passenger on his ship. She was a passenger taking a night stroll and she'd walked into harm's way because of the illegal activities of his crew.

He'd had his suspicions. He could have gone to the police in Darwin. They might not have taken his concerns seriously—what evidence did he have, other than delays and inconsistencies?—but he could have tried. Or he could have cancelled the whole cruise.

There was no use going down that road. Guilt achieved nothing.

In truth, there was no use thinking of anything. There was only the night, the sea and the touch of Rachel's hand.

The further they went, the harder it grew to fight against the current, and the last hundred or so yards to reach the island was the worst. Rachel was hardly making progress. Another woman might panic, he thought—anyone could panic right now, himself included—but there was no choice.

Head down. Stroke after stroke. Touching hands. Always touching hands.

They were fighting through breakers now. The tidal currents were fighting each other, causing a surge of white water.

Stay in contact. Stroke, stroke…

And then, magically, there was a patch of calm, where the water stilled. He looked up and saw a platform of flat rock, just out of the water as the tidal currents surged back.

A landing place.

He gripped Rachel's hand and she paused and looked up and saw what he was seeing.

Deep breath.

Head for the platform.

He reached it and hauled himself up on the rocky ledge, then turned to grasp her. They had to be together. For him to reach the ledge and lose her was unthinkable.

He had her. The current caught and tugged but he had her fast, lifting her as if she were a featherweight, up onto the rock-face and out of the sea.

He had her.

She sagged in his arms.

'Not yet, sweetheart,' he told her, harsh and loud into the night. 'Not now. We need to climb.'

He didn't say more. Exhausted or not, they had to move. Maybe she knew but, if she didn't, he wasn't telling her. Flat rock ledges on these islands were rare enough, and they were places crocodiles could use to rest or digest their kill. Or find something else to kill. A croc could launch itself at them here in an instant.

They had to get higher.

He tugged her to her feet and pulled.

'No,' she whispered.

'Yes,' he said inexorably. 'Now.'

They stumbled in the dark—of course they did. Both were barefoot. The rocks were rough and sharp but he couldn't allow her to pause. He kept the pressure on her hand and he could feel her limping. He knew her hip would be killing her, but there was nothing he could do about it. He was dragging her upward and she was doing her best to help.

And finally, finally, he found what he was looking for. A sheltered crag, high above sea level, out of the path of the wind, a ledge too far up for crocs to reach. It was dry and flat and sand covered, enough to make it softer than sheer rock.

A refuge. Safety.

The relief was almost overwhelming. He hauled her the last few steps and turned and took her into his arms. He dropped to his knees and she did the same. He held her hard against his chest and he let his chin drop onto her soaking curls.

Heartbeat to heartbeat, he simply held.

'We've made it, sweetheart,' he said at last, in a voice that was none too steady. 'We've done it. We've made it to safety.'

CHAPTER FOUR

THEY lay on the sand and they held each other.

For an hour or so they did nothing but hold each other and let the shock of the night wash over them. There was nothing sexy about the way they held; this was a simple primitive need for contact, and Finn thought at one stage maybe they would have held if they both were men.

He almost smiled at that, thinking of his manly mates, the guys who'd shared his boat-building apprenticeship. Okay, maybe they wouldn't have held, but it still would have been sensible, for what both of them needed was warmth and reassurance that the ground was solid and what had happened was real but over.

The sand still held vestiges of the sun's warmth from the day before. Under the curve of the cliff, they were protected from the night breeze. Rachel lay spooned into the curve of his body. The cold and the shock gradually eased. The warm night air enveloped them, promising a safety of its own. He held her close, murmuring words of comfort, reassurance that was as much for himself as it was for her.

After a while he realised she'd drifted into an exhausted doze, and with that came new sensations.

The feeling of protectiveness was almost overwhelming. And anger on her behalf. Here was a woman who'd been taught the hard way that bad things happened, he thought savagely, and tonight had been yet another horror.

His crew had caused it.

Thankfully, right now, her mind was shutting down, blacking out what was around and giving her time out. That was fine by him. More than fine. They'd ended up entwined on the sand, their bodies as close as they could be for maximum warmth. That was also fine. He was content to lie and wait for her to recover, and her warmth was giving him the comfort he needed as well.

There was nothing to do but try to sleep. Rescue was the last thing on his mind. A signal fire could bring—probably would bring—the very people they were trying to escape from.

So think about rescue in the morning. For now... Sleep?

Easier said than done, even when Rachel's warmth flooded him, soothed him, made the night intimate and the terrors of the past hours recede.

At one stage Rachel stirred and he felt her stiffen as memory flooded back.

'They'll come for us,' she muttered, fearful.

'No,' he said solidly, hugging her closer. 'They'll think we've drowned. Without knowledge of location and currents we couldn't have made it here.'

'How did you know...?' she whispered.

'Masculine intuition,' he murmured back, and she managed a feeble chuckle before drifting off again.

Masculine intuition. Not so much. His baggage contained detailed maps of this whole area, navigational charts, tide charts... He'd been studying them intently ever since he'd left Darwin.

They owed their lives to that knowledge—but that he'd dragged Rachel into this mess...

She'd stepped into it.

No. It was his mess.

But guilt achieved nothing. For now there was nothing to do but hold this woman close and give thanks that they were here and he had her safe.

Until morning.

They both woke fully as the first rays of dawn broke the horizon. For a while neither said anything, just savoured the stillness, the faint rising warmth and the sheer awesomeness of the place where they'd landed.

And the comfort of each other. Neither felt inclined to pull apart. Together seemed more than okay when out there was…what?

They were on a rocky outcrop rising almost sheer from the sea. In the distance—the far, far distance—was the mainland. Beyond was the horizon. A few similar outcrops were in the middle distance; the larger one they'd avoided last night was the closest but even that was far. The currents had carried them to as remote a place as they could be.

Nothing, nothing and nothing.

'Oh, my,' Rachel murmured at last. 'Where on earth are we?'

'Somewhere in the Timor Sea.'

'That's helpful.' Finally she wriggled and stirred and sat up and he was aware of a sharp stab of loss. 'Um…I'm hungry.'

Uh oh. There weren't a lot of food outlets around here.

But he might have known. Rachel wasn't complaining she was hungry because she was expecting him to do something. She was stating facts as a precursor to doing something about it herself.

'I think I still have a packet of barley sugar in my jacket pocket,' she said. 'It's zipped. You want me to see if it's still there?'

Barley sugar… Yes! 'I can't think of a better breakfast,' he told her, meaning it, and she wriggled out of his hold and undid the knot around her waist.

She'd kept hold of her jacket.

How many women would do that? he thought. How many anyones? To lie under the hull of a boat with guns above and calmly remove her jacket—and not let it drift away…

'You kept your jacket because...'

'I'm thrifty,' she said, and managed another smile. 'I paid eighty dollars for this jacket. But I'm happy to share my barley sugar.'

She was, he decided quite simply, quite definitely, quite gorgeous. She was sand and salt-coated. She was wearing a skimpy nightdress which clung transparently to her slim figure, and her curls were clinging every which way.

He'd never seen a woman so lovely.

She found her barley sugar. The wrappings were soaked but inside the sweets were fine. They sucked in contented silence, savouring the sweetness, each acknowledging the unsaid—the reason why they didn't eat half a dozen barley sugars in a row, but rather Rachel placed the rest back into her jacket pocket as if they were treasure.

'Breakfast done. Now, I wouldn't mind a bath,' she said conversationally. 'Where do you suppose the bathrooms are?'

'Behind that rock?'

'Hmm.' The thought of the promised bathrooms obviously didn't have her racing to find them. She hugged her knees and stared out at the horizon. 'Do you understand what happened last night?'

He groaned inwardly, but he knew that nothing would do but the truth.

'I suspect that was a drop-off,' he told her. 'I think the crew is smuggling drugs into Australia, and that was a transfer of drugs from Indonesia. The fact that they were prepared to kill to protect themselves says it's a huge drug haul. We walked right in on it.'

'I walked right in on it,' she said softly. 'You overheard?'

'I was on the next level up.'

'You could have gone for help,' she said, surveying him thoughtfully, thinking it through as she spoke. 'But by then I'd have been dead. You're in this mess because of me.'

'I'm in this mess because of drug runners,' he said so savagely that his words echoed out into the stillness. 'There's no blame to be laid at anyone's door, apart from those…'

'Shh.' She laid a finger on his lips, an intimate gesture that made him still. 'Don't say it. The lizards will be shocked.'

Maybe they would. He followed her gaze and

saw a host of tiny skinks emerging out from the shadows to catch the first rays of the morning sun.

'This is Robinson Crusoe territory,' she said, and amazingly he saw laughter lurking in those gorgeous brown eyes. 'I bet these guys have never met anything even vaguely like us. You want their first experience of humankind to be guys muttering oaths?'

'Maybe we need to parley with the natives,' he agreed. 'Trade. You think they'd be interested in our barley sugar wrappers?'

'In exchange for what?'

'Water would be good.'

'Water would be excellent,' she agreed. 'How lucky I brought my rain jacket.'

'Um…' He thought about that for a moment, looking at it from all angles. 'You're planning a war dance?'

'No, but I can make a still.'

'A what?'

'A water still. We need a nice scoopy hollow,' she said, and amazingly she sounded enthusiastic. 'In full sun. And then we find a hollowed rock or something that can fit in the middle to be used as a container. The idea is we pack around the container with anything green—there's enough plant life here to use. Then we cover the whole lot with my waterproof jacket. We weigh it down and the heat makes the plants sweat. The water collects on the plastic and runs down into the container. It works a treat.'

'How do you know this?' he said faintly.

'I'm a geologist. I've never been stuck for water but the first time I was ever out in the field our instructor showed us how to do it. Just in case. It's neat.'

'And that's why you hung onto your jacket,' he managed, stunned.

She smiled at that, and looked a bit embarrassed.

'Um…apart from not wanting to lose my eighty dollars, that would also be modesty,' she conceded. 'I know, it was really dumb when people were shooting at us, but this nightie is really skimpy.'

'I'd noticed,' he admitted, and she glared.

'Well, stop noticing. I don't even have any kn…' She stopped mid-word and she turned bright, glorious pink. 'Just stop noticing,' she repeated and he thought, she's gorgeous. She's plain, unarguably gorgeous.

He'd been ordered not to notice. How was a man not to notice?

He was still wearing trousers and a T-shirt. He was relatively respectable. Rachel's nightdress, on the other hand, was of the flimsiest cotton and it wasn't respectable at all.

And she wasn't wearing any kn…

How was a man not to notice?

But she'd stopped thinking of her appearance. 'Do you think they'll come looking for us?' she asked, and he knew that, despite the distractions, fear was still front and centre. Their moment of shared humour died.

'No,' he said, and he put everything he knew how into making that word absolute.

Her face changed, just a little but enough for him to know his authority had sunk home.

'How can you be sure?'

'Esme and her crew decided not to do a full scale search last night. If they had, there'd have been lights on, searchlights, tenders out, all of which we'd have still been within distance to hear and see. They won't know that I know the currents and tides, which means they'll assume we've drowned. Their plan must be to simply go about their business and wait for us to be missed.' He glanced at his watch. 'Which won't even be yet. It's not breakfast time and unless you and Maud meet before breakfast...'

'We don't.'

'Then no one will realise we're missing until then. By the time they do, the *Temptress* could be almost a hundred miles from where we are now. And the boat that dropped the drugs won't be Australian. They have nothing to gain and everything to lose by spending time searching for people who are Esme's problem, not theirs.'

'So we wait to be rescued by the good guys,' she said in a small voice.

'Yes,' he agreed but he didn't get the inflexion right because Rachel looked at him sharply.

'You don't think that'll happen?'

'Of course it will.'

But...

But this place was like a giant haystack, and they were a needle. The resources needed to search an area as remote as this were enormous. How many choppers could be brought from Darwin or Broome—and how likely was it that the authorities would hold out any hope for them at all? There'd be a token search, he thought, but the search area was vast. He and Rachel could have come off the ship any time between supper and breakfast. The area to be searched would be thousands of square miles.

'Well, you don't need to fret,' Rachel said, and this time she was doing the comforting. 'Maud will find us. Though I hate to think of her stuck on that ship with those creeps.'

'They'll hardly harm any more of the passengers,' he told her. 'Maud's safe. But as for helping us…'

'If you think my Maud will leave this to the authorities, you have another think coming,' she said and, amazingly, her smile had returned. 'I've seen Maud in action and I know what she's capable of. I'm lucky enough to call her my friend, and she doesn't lose friends lightly. She and her grandson run Thurston Holdings, and they have mines all through the northern outback. I'm guessing the entire Thurston workforce will be redirected into saving a couple of bedraggled strays before the breakfast coffee's served on the *Temptress*.'

'But you said yourself,' Finn said faintly. 'You only met the lady three weeks ago.'

'Maud loves me,' Rachel said. 'That'll do it.'

'After three weeks?'

'Don't you dare sound derisive,' she snapped. 'Maud's fabulous.'

'But loving after three weeks...'

'How long do you think it takes to love someone?'

'I wouldn't know. But you don't even know someone in three weeks.'

'What about your parents?' she asked, and he thought, she's using this as a way to stop thinking about where we are for a moment. She's giving herself time out. 'How long did they know each other before they...?'

'They knew each other for a week,' he snapped, because suddenly he couldn't help himself. He didn't tell people this. He barely told himself, yet here was this waif of a woman, blindly believing in love at first sight, and she needed to be set straight now. 'They were together for a week. I was conceived and they never saw each other again. Three weeks to love? I'd need three years more likely, and even then I'd want references.'

'Oh, Finn...'

'And the father of your baby?' he demanded, still angry. Maybe the tension of the night had got to him in a way that was doing something to his head—demanding honesty from himself as well as from her.

'That was a mistake, too,' she whispered. 'So maybe your three-year rule's better. Maybe that's what I should hang onto.' She bit her lip and closed her eyes—but then she opened them and she was resolute again. 'But, sensible or not, loving is what Maud does, and she loves me and she'll search for me, and so will my sister, Amy, and my brother-in-law-to-be, Hugo. They'll find me. And you? Will your family help?'

'No.' How to tell her his family—Connie and Richard—didn't even know where he was, or that he was travelling under a false name. They shared a house but they didn't live in each other's pockets. He'd told them he was going away for work, and had left it at that.

If he didn't get home he'd left instructions with

his lawyers. Maybe they'd be a bit upset, but they were provided for.

They'd be okay—but he'd prefer the lawyer's instructions weren't needed, he conceded. Especially if it meant a pile of bleached bones lying on some deserted island.

Love or not, Rachel's Maud was looking a good option, he conceded. Maybe Rachel was right. From what he'd seen of Maud, no matter if the *Temptress*'s crew was saying they'd both been seen eaten by crocodiles, she'd be scouring the sea looking for crocs to hold accountable.

She loved Rachel.

The thought was weirdly unsettling and, on a morning when his thoughts should be focused anywhere else, he was suddenly thinking of affection and how rare it was, and how could an elderly lady possibly love a young woman after three weeks' acquaintance?

He glanced at Rachel and thought...love?

And then he thought, that nightdress is way too sheer and this island is far too small.

She caught his gaze—and firmly hauled her jacket over her salt-encrusted nightdress and did up the buttons.

'You'll be hot.'

'I'm not hot,' she said firmly, definitely, and it was as much as he could do not to refute it and tell her how hot she actually was. But a man had some sense of self-preservation. 'We need to find water, loner boy,' she snapped. 'Much as my water-making ability is awesome, it's slow. The water I can make should help us survive but not much more, and we'd look a bit silly if there's a waterfall just behind that rock.'

'And it rained here two days ago.'

'How do you know that?' she demanded, astounded.

'Weather forecast. I've been watching the whole route on the Internet.'

'The ship's Internet's been out of order.'

It had. That was another thing that made him suspicious. Esme and her crew had obviously taken precautions. The Internet failing was just one more minor hiccup that plagued the cruise, annoying the passengers, but it meant that if anyone had seen anything suspicious there'd be no way of contacting the authorities. Except using the ship's radio.

The Captain allowed the radio to be used for

urgent contact home, but the times had to be booked in advance, and he was always within earshot.

The Captain must be in on this. He was starting to see the whole set-up, and it made him feel ill.

But now wasn't the time for thinking about what had happened. Rachel was looking at him with speculation. 'You know the currents and tides. You know the islands and you know the weather.'

'I'm travelling by myself. I have…' Why not say it? 'I have satellite connection in my cabin and I have time to trawl the Internet.'

'You're not an undercover policeman, are you?'

That caught him. This lady was smart. 'No,' he managed.

She gave him another thoughtful glance, almost disbelieving, but then obviously decided not to pursue it. 'What a shame,' she said, obviously making an effort to keep it light. 'If I've been caught up in an undercover drug bust…if you were official I might be able to sue the government.'

'You might be able to sue the cruise line.'

'There is that,' she said, brightening. 'I'll have my lawyers look into it. Meanwhile, water.'

'Yes, ma'am,' he said and they went to search.

They found three pools of fresh water, two only three or four inches deep but wide—maybe four feet or so—the other only eighteen inches wide but maybe two feet deep.

At the sight of them Rachel gave a sob of relief and knelt to scoop a drink from the deepest.

He stopped her before she touched it.

'Sense here,' he told her. The deep pool was the run-off from a couple of smooth rocks sloped above. It was the most secure of the water sources.

By the look of the other two, they'd almost evaporated. The day promised to be hot and clear and they were in full sun. Shallow and wide… Another day like yesterday and they'd be gone by day's end.

He needed to think this through.

They were both desperately thirsty. Their faces were salt encrusted—they were totally salt-encrusted—but who knew how long they'd be stuck here?

'We can live for weeks without food,' he said, still gripping her. 'But not without water and there's no forecast for rain in the foreseeable future.'

'Are we thinking weeks?' Rachel said in a small voice. 'My barley sugar won't last.'

'Hey, we can always eat each other,' he said grandly, as if he were offering her a degustation menu at the world's best restaurant, and she glanced up at him and he smiled and she managed a smile back.

'So... We're planning on drawing straws?'

'I'm voting the lizards get it before we do,' he said, mock grave. 'I'm also depending on your Maud that we don't go past barley sugar, but it's going to be hot today and water's vital.'

'So our plan is?' Rachel said, looking longingly into the depths of the little pool.

'We drink now from the shallow pools, then we work fast to preserve as much as we can before they evaporate,' Finn said. 'We can use your jacket to scoop water from the shallow pools to the bigger pool. Then we cover the deep pool with your jacket so it doesn't evaporate.'

'You want me to take my jacket off again,' she

said and sighed, but she was already undoing the buttons. 'Okay, this might be flimsy but you get any ideas, I'll report you straight to Dame Maud, nerd boy.'

'Nerd boy?'

'Anyone who spends a cruise like this in his cabin studying charts and weather forecasts and currents, and isn't a policeman doing it for good, has to be a nerd. I bet you play Dungeons and Dragons on the side. I'm stuck on a desert island with a geek.' Sigh. 'How do we shift this water?'

'We use your sleeves,' he told her and, before she could object, he'd ripped off a sleeve and knotted it firmly to make a long, narrow bag. Then she watched as he started scooping the water into his 'bag' from the shallow pools and carrying it to the deeper pool.

She stood back, impressed. This man was purposeful and clever. Maud might be in the background as her saviour but Finn was here and now.

She set to work with the other sleeve. Their deep hole grew deeper.

They worked for fifteen minutes, getting every drop of water they could from both pools. Finally they'd scooped all they could—the water was too shallow to scoop more. Finn covered the deep pool with the body of Rachel's jacket, weighed it down with rocks and then looked up at her and smiled.

'Now the reward,' he said softly, motioning to the remnants of the shallow pools. 'We can't get the last inch from either. As soon as the sun gets some heat, it'll be gone. How about a bath each?'

A bath. Oh, my.

'One each,' he said and she closed her eyes in bliss.

She had a nice flat plane of clear water. It might only be an inch or so deep but it was hers. All hers.

Finn could do what he liked with his but she knew what she was doing with hers.

She lay and drank as much as she could, and then she washed her face, and then, because she knew there was no way she could do this again—from now on the precious deep hole must be for drinking only—she decided to be really indulgent.

It wouldn't work if she kept her nightie on, she thought. The water wasn't deep enough. But she could take the garment off and rinse it in the remnants—and then she could wallow herself, all over.

The thought of getting the salt from her skin was irresistible.

'Turn the other way,' she told Finn, who washing his face in his pool.

'Sorry?'

'This is my bath,' she declared. 'It might be a while until I see another so I'm making the most of it. Don't you dare look. But if you do the same in your pool I promise not to look at you either. If we take it in turns I suspect we'll lose even more from evaporation and I'm not waiting one minute.'

He looked at her.

'Look away,' she ordered—and he turned.

Trust him, she told herself and, for some reason, she did. Honourable scoundrel. Nerd boy. The guy who'd saved her life.

She slipped off her nightdress and she lay full length in the shallow pool. She rolled and she rolled and then—as much as anyone could in an inch of water—she wallowed.

She splayed her curls out and ran her fingers through them over and over. The pool was uneven so there were deeper dips—there was enough water here to make this work.

'Good?' Finn asked in a voice that sounded strangled.

'Heaven.' She dared a glance back at him. 'Why aren't you doing the same? You're wasting time.'

She could see him tense. She could feel him tense. Maybe she was testing the honourable scoundrel too far.

'I'm not looking,' she said, and deliberately turned away from looking at that broad back, the thick thatch of hair that made her think of running her fingers through it…

Whoa? Who was the scoundrel here?

She rolled to her side and deliberately turned her back on him.

Ten seconds later, she heard him roll into the water and she knew he was doing the same.

It would have been fine except for the eagle. Or osprey.

One minute she was splashing the cool, clear water over and over her body. The next the bird swept down from nowhere, a vast black shadow, blocking the sun, screeching from the heights, talons outstretched, straight towards her.

'Rachel, duck!' Finn's words were a roar.

Did she scream? She had no idea. All she knew was that one minute she was soaking in sun and water and safety, the next she was over in Finn's pool, closer to the cliff, grabbed, held, rolled out of the pool and under the shelter of the cliff face.

Then held until the giant shadow wheeled and retreated and there was nothing but clear sky.

'It's gone,' Finn said, and she heard herself whimper.

What a baby—yet she couldn't stop herself shaking.

She was safe, yet still he held her, and still she needed to be held.

She was wet and warm and safe—and totally naked.

So was he.

She didn't care. The terror of the night before and the fear of not being found combined. Simple overwhelming fear was all around her, and this man and his body were the only things between her and terror.

And he held her as she needed to be held, tight and hard and strong, and, she thought afterwards, maybe he was taking comfort as well as giving.

If he hadn't yelled... If he hadn't grabbed her...

'Hey, that was a surprise,' he said at last, thickly into her hair, not letting her go an inch. 'I didn't realise we had company. I'm thinking there's an osprey's nest on top of our island. Should we call *National Geographic*?'

An osprey's nest...

Her mind clicked from fear to logic. What Finn was saying made sense. She'd seen the giant ospreys during the cruise, their massive nests perched on the highest spots of the most inaccessible crags, where the birds could watch the world while they raised their young.

'You don't mess with those guys,' Jason had said when he'd pointed out the first one she'd seen, and she knew he was right.

'Would...' She could barely get the words out. 'Would it have attacked?'

'We're too big for them to do much damage,'

Finn said. 'That guy was on a scare mission, not a breakfast mission.'

'That makes me feel better,' she managed un-convincingly.

'Me, too,' he said, just as unconvincingly, and he held her closer still while her heart regained its rhythm and she remembered again how to breathe.

And she felt his breathing.

And she felt how solid he was, and how smooth his bare back was and how strong were the rip-ples of the muscles across his shoulders.

This guy was seriously ripped.

Maybe he had a gym in that baggage of his, she decided. A gym was about the only luxury the *Temptress* didn't provide—the daily activi-ties more than made up for it.

Um… She was fighting for sanity here. What was she thinking? Whether or not the *Temptress* had a gym, when she was being held by a guy who felt…who felt…

'Better?' he asked gently and she managed to nod, but she didn't let go.

'We'll stay under the shelter of the cliffs,' he said. 'We need to anyway, now the sun has some strength, and if we don't climb higher she'll stop seeing us as a threat.'

'G…great.'

'Rachel?'

'M…mmm?'

He cupped her chin and he forced her to look out to sea. 'See that island over there?'

The crag he was pointing to was high and wide, covered with straggly trees and surrounded by reefs. It was half a mile away.

For the rest…she could see maybe a hundred small rocky outcrops like this one. This was a vast ocean of islands, with the mainland far away in the distance.

'That island was closest to us last night,' Finn said gently. 'If Esme wanted to search, she'd have gone there. Unlikely, but if she did…it'd take half a day to search it. But they're on the cruise ship and they need to pretend they know nothing about what happened to us. The guys who did the drop won't search. As for here… The osprey's protecting her babies and nothing else. If we leave her alone, she'll leave us alone. We're clean, we have water, we have barley sugar, and somewhere out there we have your Maud, regimenting the troops. We *are* safe.'

And, for the first time, she believed him.

Safe. It was a weird way of describing where they were now, she thought. On a barren outcrop in the middle of nowhere, completely stranded. But the overriding fear of whoever it was coming back…he'd just taken it away. She sagged against him and he held.

He swore and kissed her gently on her hair.

'You're done, sweetheart,' he said, and she hauled herself away at that. But not very far because if she hauled away more than three inches she saw all of him, and somehow it seemed safer to stay close. And…better.

He swore again and tugged her to his heart.

'I'm not done,' she managed, trying to sound indignant. 'Or no more done than you are.'

'Which is why I need to keep holding you.' She could hear the smile in his voice, and it settled her still more. But it made her feel…it made her feel…

As if she were being cradled by a totally naked guy with laughter in his voice.

'I don't need to be held,' she said but her heart wasn't in it.

'But you'd like to be held?'

'I…yes.' There was no denying such a truth.

There was a moment's stillness. And then…

'I'd like to kiss you,' he said, and her heart seemed to falter.

'Really?' she said because she couldn't think of anything else to say.

And then, because she couldn't think of any better response, she went for the obvious.

'So what's stopping you?'

CHAPTER FIVE

As a response, it took Finn's breath right away.

He was holding a naked woman in his arms, and she was encouraging him to kiss her.

To comfort her?

Maybe that was it, he thought. Maybe he could keep comforting her by continuing to hold her.

But she'd agreed with the idea—in principle— of kissing.

So in practice…

Enough of the thoughts. Right there, right then, body took over brain. He had an unimaginably beautiful woman naked in his arms, and she was asking to be kissed. A man'd have to be inhuman…

He wasn't inhuman.

They were a man and a woman and there was nothing in the world between them.

He gazed down at her in the shadowed light in the lee of the cliffs—and he kissed her.

* * *

Rachel Cotton hadn't been kissed for a very long time.

Ramón didn't count. Her ex-husband was a lying, cheating toe rag and she'd blocked out his kisses as something she never had to think of again.

Excluding Ramón, she hadn't been kissed since she was at university. Which was a long time ago.

She was making up for it now, because Finn Kinnard's mouth met hers and fire met fire.

She didn't know she could burn until he kissed her. She didn't know a body could.

His mouth claimed hers, she clung to his wet, naked body, she let herself be kissed, she kissed him right back—and it felt like her world was melting.

The heat started in her mouth and in her hands where she held him and clung, but it spread outward, up, down, a slow, deep flame that grew and grew and consumed her to the point where she felt she was melting into this man.

Two becoming one? She'd heard the analogy— wasn't it in the marriage vows?—but she'd never known it for truth before. But that was what this felt like.

She kissed and let herself be kissed. She clung and she forgot everything but this man, this body.

She let herself simply cling…

The kiss extended. They were using it to forget, to take and give comfort, to replace fear with a need as old as time itself.

It was working. All she could think of was his body.

All she could think of was this kiss.

Finn. Boat-builder. A man who knew how to wield tools. Irresistably, toe-curlingly sexy.

But also…an investigator?

Then, out of nowhere, something more.

He had kids.

Children.

The knowledge slammed into her consciousness, piercing the dream quality of what was happening as if a sledgehammer had sliced down, straight through the mist of emotion, fear and sheer raw need.

This was a guy she knew nothing about. He had kids who he'd presumably left with their mother. Or mothers. She was kissing him as if she'd sink into him. If he had condoms on his naked person, the way she was feeling, she'd melt.

Maybe it was that tiny thought—had he remembered to pack condoms?—the almost hysterical idiocy of the idea—that made her acknowledge reality. Reason.

Reason tasted sour and empty when all she wanted, all she needed, was to hold and keep on holding, but somehow she managed to stiffen, to tug away—and she was released in an instant.

'We…can't,' she said, and there was no way on earth she could keep the regret and longing from her voice.

What was it with her? She'd fallen for Ramón in just such a heat. She'd wanted him and she'd put logic aside and she'd fallen.

She'd known Ramón had an ego. She'd known that he drank, but she'd figured he controlled the drinking enough to dance at the highest level; he could control it to love her.

Only she hadn't been important enough.

Like she wasn't important to this man. This

man who'd already warned her of his past, his reputation.

His honour?

Yes, he was honourable, for he was putting her away from him, his gaze as rueful, as regretful as hers.

'I guess…not the best idea,' he managed. 'If we're stuck here for nine months, there's nowhere to buy bootees.'

She managed a laugh that was almost a sob, and he raised his hands and cupped her face, his fingers strong and firm and tender all at once.

'But it won't be nine months,' he said. 'We depend on your Maud, and I'm sure you're right. She'll be here. So now…we put on our nice clean clothes, we make ourselves as respectable as we can and we wait for the cavalry.'

'You're sure it won't be…?'

'It won't be anyone but Maud,' he said, and she met his gaze and she believed him.

They were safe—or as safe as stuck on a deserted island hundreds of miles from anywhere with nothing but a limited amount of water and half a bag of barley sugar could make them.

'Do you think Maud will know to pack condoms?' Finn asked, and she choked and laughed and it was okay again. Sort of.

'I wonder how lizards taste roasted,' Finn continued, diving out of the shadows to retrieve their clothing. He was back before their friend from above could realise he was out there, handing her her nightdress and calmly hauling on his wet trousers. 'We might have to find out.'

'Roast lizard,' she said, trying to sound thoughtful, trying to sound calm and sensible as she tugged her nightdress back on and wished fiercely that she was wearing flannelette pyjamas instead of the wisp of frivolity her sister had given her when she was in hospital. 'Do you have a box of matches and a fry pan in your pocket?' Then she glanced at his trousers—and looked away. Uh oh. Her face turned bright pink.

They really had been very close to…to…

To needing an airdrop of condoms.

'I do have something that'll help,' he said gravely, and he tugged forward a small, waterproof pouch that had been attached to his belt. 'I know I should have packed it with more barley sugar—remiss on my part—but it's what I always carry in here.'

He flicked it open, revealing a phone-cum-camera—and a solid all purpose knife.

'The advertisement for this knife says it's all you need to survive the end of the world,' he said. 'Let's see if it works.'

'The phone...' she said with longing, looking at what she most wanted in the world. Communication.

'I haven't had a signal for days,' he told her. 'Sadly, my satellite phone's back on the ship. I've been using this little sucker for other things.' He flicked the phone open and showed her, and she thought he was doing it to distract her. He was showing her the phone so she could stop thinking about what had just happened, about what so nearly had continued to happen, and that he was so male and so near and so...so...

'Pictures,' he said and she thought—almost hysterically—is he going to show me pictures of his kids?

But no.

He gestured to a ledge and they sat—like two acquaintances meeting over morning coffee—and he showed her what he had.

He had pictures of the aft deck of the boat,

taken at night. The only light was one being held by one of the deckhands as Esme leaned down to retrieve parcels.

There were a dozen photographs, one after the other, culminating in the parcel tossed onto the deck, the powder spreading. In the last blurry shot she could see a fuzzy shape at the edge of the shot—which was her walking right in.

'Thank God this pouch is waterproof. When Maud comes, these guys will pay,' Finn said grimly. 'I promise you. This is enough evidence to put them away for years. But meanwhile, let's think about fire.'

'Fire?'

'Roast lizards.'

'You're serious?'

'If we must.'

'My grandmother said they taste okay,' she said, and that caught him.

'Your grandma?'

'Her people come from the Alice. Near Uluru. She spent her childhood in the bush.'

'She didn't give you cooking lessons, I suppose?'

'Not exactly lizards.'

'Then we do it from scratch,' he said. 'And we start now. I suspect the old idea of rubbing two sticks together to make a fire could take a while. We need to get it done by tonight, though. And somehow I need to get up top to make a signal. That'll be my T-shirt.'

'You're going to wave your T-shirt?'

'Your nightie would be better,' he said and he grinned. 'But you've already donated your jacket and I suspect any more donations might be above and beyond the call of duty.'

'Yes,' she said faintly. 'Um…the ospreys?'

'We watch Mummy and Daddy Osprey and, the moment they're both out hunting, up I go, with you as lookout. And if they even think about coming back, you yell and I'll run away. I'm very good at running away. It's one of my principal skills.'

She looked at him, seeing humour in his face, but also strength and resolution and courage.

He was planning out loud to reassure her, she thought, and it was working.

She didn't think he was very good at running away at all.

Children or not, scoundrel or not, she could depend on this guy. She would depend on him. She just…wouldn't do anything else.

CHAPTER SIX

'I'M AFRAID it's obvious.'

Maud was staring down at Rachel's slipper. The Captain was holding it out as if it explained all, and it explained nothing. She glared at the officer in front of her, her fear compressed into a ball of tightly contained fury.

'If it's obvious, why aren't I seeing it? Explain?'

'The crew found this on the top deck at dawn, plus empty champagne bottles. We believe your companion and Mr Kinnard have had some kind of late night assignation. Esme, our chief tour leader, saw them up there a few nights ago and warned them, but obviously they didn't listen. The water was choppy last night and the ship hit a couple of large, sharp swells as the tide turned. If they were drunk...I'm very sorry, Dame Maud, but we're looking at tragedy. Of course I'll notify the authorities. They'll run a sweep over the entire area...'

'What manpower?' Maud demanded and he blinked.

'Excuse me?'

'How many aircraft can we get here?'

'I'm not sure...'

'Well, get sure,' she snapped. 'And I need access to your radio straight away.'

'Dame Maud, we'll do all we can.'

'You do that,' she said almost cordially. 'And I'll add all I can on top of it. But let's get one thing clear. My Rachel did not fall from this ship in a fit of drunken passion. And you can cut your search area down as well. Rachel went to bed when I did, and she always goes straight to sleep. It's hours later that the nightmares start. I'm thinking she went overboard some time after two and before four.'

'How can you...?'

'Because that's when she's awake,' she snapped. 'So I need the coordinates of exactly where we were at two and exactly where we were at four.'

'I'll give you our exact route.'

'I'm not interested in your exact route,' she

snapped, and for a moment she sounded the frightened old lady she was. 'I want proof of where you were at two and proof of where you were at four and I'll take it from there. Or my grandson will. They will be found.'

'I hate to mention it, but ma'am, the crocs and sharks in this water...'

'I know exactly what lives in these waters,' she snapped. 'But if you think I'm searching for what's left of Rachel, you have another think coming. And if you think I'm swallowing that nonsense about a romantic tryst...I wish it could be true but this is Rachel we're talking about and she has no time for anybody.'

Esme was fully occupied. She was intent on organising the next shore trip, pushing the events of the night before to one side. No matter what had happened, the rest of the passengers had to be catered for.

Things were going well. Settling down. It had been explained to the *Temptress*'s crew and passengers that there'd been a tragic incident in the night. The passengers had been warned yet again of the dangers of excess drinking on deck. Although some were visibly upset, most were thinking *Young fools—and let's get on; the authorities will deal with it.*

'Should we worry?'

Esme turned and frowned her displeasure. The engineer shouldn't be up on this deck. They needed to make everything look normal; she let her annoyance show.

'There's no need,' she said brusquely. 'You took the tender around the only habitable island and saw nothing. We were miles off course. The crocs will have finished our business nicely.'

'Should we get rid of the stuff?'

'Will you shut up?' she hissed. 'I told you, there's no need. I don't intend to take all that risk for nothing.'

'But if they're found… They'll have guessed exactly what we were doing.'

'Who's going to find them out here? They're finished. We have nothing to worry about. Get back to where you belong. They're nothing but a tragic accident that's past and done with.'

Not quite. It was eight in the morning when Hugo Thurston took the call—and by eight fifteen every resource of Thurston Holdings was diverted to looking for one girl who'd fallen off a ship somewhere between Darwin and Broome, and the guy who'd fallen off with her.

'He'd better look after her.' Amy, Rachel's sister, was helpless in her terror when Hugo broke the news.

'If I know the Cotton women, it'll be the other way round,' Hugo said grimly. 'Heaven help anything that threatens our Rachel.'

'If he tried to attack her... If that's why she fell...'

'Then he'll be croc meat and she'll be sitting on a rock somewhere waiting for us to fetch her,' he said. 'So let's not mess around. Let's get your sister rescued.'

CHAPTER SEVEN

'I DON'T suppose you thought to pack a Scrabble board in your waterproof pouch,' Rachel said.

It was three o'clock. The heat outside the shelter of their rock ledge was searing. The last of their shallow rock pools had long dried up and only the makeshift cover over the deeper hole was protecting their water.

She'd like another drink but it was too hot to head out and get one. Why couldn't the waterhole be in the shade?

Why couldn't lots of things?

There were too many questions and no answers at all.

'Scrabble,' Finn said cautiously. 'Sorry, I forgot.'

'It would have been useful. Even a pack of cards...'

'I always was useless at packing.'

She managed a smile at his contrition.

They were sitting as far back in the shadows

as they could manage. Maybe they should be down on the shore, waving for help.

Not yet. There'd be crocs on the shoreline and they had a decent lookout here.

They needed to get the T-shirt up the scree—but there was a problem. The rock was brittle and crumbling, and every time the birds took off and Finn tried to climb, he ended up crumbling the edges still more and making no progress.

Rachel had been gearing up for an hour now. Thinking…could she?

She and Amy had spent their childhood becoming seriously good at martial arts. She'd also done serious gym work getting her hip back to strength. It meant she was agile and fast. Also light.

She still had a gammy hip. It still didn't do what it was supposed to do. If Finn knew how badly it was damaged…

He didn't, and the only way to get the T-shirt up there was for her to get it there.

She sat and thought about Scrabble for a while and thought about water and the rest of the barley sugar.

She tried not to think about the guy beside her, who'd grown silent as well.

He was carving something out of a piece of wood he'd found, whittling with patience, intent on who knew what?

She was so aware of him…

The second osprey launched itself from the nest and headed out to sea. The first had gone five minutes before.

They'd been timing the birds. Each excursion lasted half an hour or more.

They had twenty-five minutes. *She had twenty-five minutes.*

She pushed herself to her feet. 'T-shirt.'

He stared up at her, startled. 'What?'

'I'm climbing. Give it to me.'

'You know we can't.' He spoke as if he were humouring a child. 'I've tried. It's too dangerous.'

'Not to me. I'm light, lithe and strong.'

'You have a bad leg.'

'I *had* a bad leg, and I've been climbing since I was a kid. Anything there was to climb, I've climbed. I've also been on more geology excursions than you've had hot dinners and I know my rocks. I know what's stable and what's not. While you've been whittling your tourist carvings...'

'Tourist carvings...' He almost exploded. 'You think I'm carving...what, wooden crocodiles?'

'I'm sure they'll turn out very pretty,' she said placatingly, 'but I've been looking up at the crag, figuring out a route. I have it worked out. T-shirt. I'm going now.'

He put down his carving. 'You're not going anywhere.'

'Says who?'

'Rachel...'

'We have no choice. Field glasses will never pick us from a distance.' She held out her hand for the shirt. 'You know that. A T-shirt waving from the top may well do the trick. You're wasting time. Hand it over.'

'You'll kill yourself. No.'

'If I don't go, we may well both starve to death, and you know that, too. I won't kill myself, and I need to go—now.'

'We'll both...'

'You're not coming,' she snapped. 'You'll crumple my rock.'

'Heaven forbid. So I stand at the bottom and catch?'

'I won't fall.'

There was a moment's silence. A moment's tense battle of wills.

'Then I'll stand at the bottom and watch you not fall,' he said at last. 'And watch for ospreys.'

'Thank you,' she said, and went.

To say he was astounded would be an understatement. He, Finn Kinnard, was standing at the base of a crumbling cliff, while a little cute woman was scaling the cliff above him—doing what had to be done to get them rescued.

To say Finn had a warped view of women would be unfair. Or would it?

To say Finn had a warped view of small, cute women would be fairer.

It was, in fact, not fair at all, but it was true.

His mother had been small and cute. She'd also been a victim, a doormat, who'd depended on his grandfather for everything. Her ill health had excused her—a bit—but Finn's grandmother had been the same.

Rachel Cotton was small and cute—and she

was halfway up a jutting crag in the middle of nowhere, when any minute the ospreys could return and she'd be in deathly trouble.

'I won't be,' she'd said. 'You watch for them, you yell and I'll scramble down so fast you won't see me for dust.'

Which would work if she was only halfway up, but if she was any further...

She carried a stick, the heaviest she could find, strapped to her shoulder by his belt. She could defend herself but these birds were huge.

He watched her climb, he saw the hesitation every time she put weight on her left hip, he saw resolution in every fibre of her body, and he thought... He thought...

He thought she might as well be a six foot six Amazonian. One of those mythical women who chopped a breast off to give them better aim for their arrows.

Something was twisting inside him. Changing.

Swimming with her last night, there'd been no hint of clinging. No hesitation. She'd twisted her jacket off and knotted it, thinking for herself, and then she'd swum at his side, asking nothing of him but that he stay beside her—and he'd asked that of her as well.

This morning she'd reacted in fear when the osprey swooped, and she'd clung, but then she'd pulled away. Since then she'd been entirely practical. She'd made herself as respectable as she could. She'd been prosaic and sensible, timing the ospreys, watching as he'd attempted to climb, watching as he'd failed.

All the time assessing her own chances.

That was why he was letting her go. He could see her mind working. As he'd failed the first time she hadn't said, *Let me try.* She'd watched him fail again—and again—because for him to climb was the most sensible option. He was stronger and he didn't have an injured hip.

But then she'd sat and thought and assessed the crag and come to her own conclusion.

Which made him think… Maybe he shouldn't be quite as definite in his classification of little cute women.

Maybe he should reclassify Rachel.

Maybe he already had.

And maybe there were other things than her courage that were changing that classification as well. The way she looked… The way she felt in his arms…

Holding her, wet and naked in the pool, feeling her heartbeat against his, feeling her mould to him… Watching her now, clambering resolutely upward, he felt…

Okay, he didn't know what he felt. He was feeling emotions he didn't recognise.

Which wasn't surprising, given the circumstances, he thought dryly, but this was more than that.

He wanted…

No. This was not the time to think about wanting Rachel Cotton.

She'd reached the top. He could only watch her out of the corner of his eye because all his attention had to be on the skyline, watching for the ospreys returning.

They'd agreed she'd drape the shirt over the topmost rock and weight a corner, so it'd flap in the breeze.

Instead she hauled the stick from her belt, tied the shirt to the end—a simple rip in the sleeve had it attached like a flag—shoved it into a fissure in the rock and turned to come down.

As a dark shape appeared on the horizon.

'Rachel…'

'I'm on my way…' She was already slithering and he swore.

'The stick…' He was yelling now. She needed it—that's why she'd taken it—but she'd left it behind to get the shirt higher.

He couldn't get up there to help her. The rock crumbled under his weight—he tried again and the weathered edges simply gave.

'Hurry…' It was a desperate roar.

'Believe it or not…' Unbelievably there was laughter in her reply as she called down to him. 'I'm hurrying.'

Not fast enough. The bird had seen Rachel, was screeching in, fast and furious…

Finn launched a rock straight up.

It didn't hit—of course it didn't—but it was enough to make the osprey veer and circle and come round again.

Another rock was hurled upward as Rachel clambered on.

Another.

Another.

And then she was on the final rock, shoulder

height, close enough for him to grab her and lift her and haul her back into the shadows of the cliff and hold her safe.

And hold her and hold her while he rethought this attitude to women in general and this woman in particular and maybe his attitude to all women in the known universe.

Or just one.

Rachel.

She didn't stay in his arms for her. She did it for him.

She'd figured it out. She'd fallen into him in terror this morning but this was different.

He was the one who'd been frightened, she thought. He was the one who needed reassurance. She was doing him a favour letting him hold her, and that was the only reason she was still here.

She had no business thinking how good it felt and how safe and how warm and how...right.

Be practical, she told herself. Move on.

He was still holding her. She could feel his heartbeat.

Move on.

Her feet hurt. That was something a girl could safely think about.

'My feet hurt,' she said, muffled against his breast, and she felt him think about it. He hugged her close one last, long time—and finally, reluctantly—really reluctantly—put her away from him. Not far. Just at arm's length.

'Your feet…'

'I needed hobnail boots.'

They both did. He'd abandoned his shoes in the swim last night and she hadn't been wearing any. His feet were raw and bleeding from his attempts to climb the crag, and he didn't have dainty female feet.

Only he had to stop that sort of thinking. He was starting to figure out that thinking of Rachel as dainty was just plain wrong.

'Let's see,' he said, and she plopped down on the rock and checked them out.

He stared down at her, at this fragile-looking slip of a woman who'd just climbed a crag he couldn't, who'd risked her neck by making their flag more obvious, who was now sitting cross-legged, studying the soles of her feet.

'Ouch,' she said. 'Do yours look like this?'

She saw his answer on his face and she winced.

'And you tried three times!'

'And you tried once and succeeded.'

'Yeah, and now I can't even whinge to you,' she said mournfully.

'But you can look at your flag.'

'I can,' she said and cheered up. They could see it from where they sheltered, a brave little flag fluttering in the hot wind. 'Unless the ospreys attack it.'

'They're too busy worrying about you.'

'They'll get used to us.' She sighed. 'I'd give anything to stick these feet in our waterhole.'

'It'd add flavour.'

She grinned. 'Ugh. You want a barley sugar?'

'It's been hours since breakfast,' he conceded. 'We might as well make pigs of ourselves.'

'Let's do it,' she said, and they ceremoniously unwrapped a barley sugar apiece and then sat side by side and looked out at the endless ocean and their little flag, and all sorts of thoughts were going through both of their minds but neither could find the courage to say any of them.

Rachel finally figured what it was Finn had been whittling. He'd carved a slot six inches long and an inch wide in a flat piece of driftwood, and then made a rounded stick, eight inches long and a fraction thinner than the slot. He proceeded to rub the stick back and forth in the slot, methodically, patiently, over and over, with his arms in the sun to get maximum heat. He was making a fire.

'I read about this somewhere,' he told her. 'It's more effective than rubbing two sticks together. Or it should be.'

She watched for a while, fascinated. She offered to help but he knocked her back.

'This is man's work.'

'So we're dividing labour according to sex? You want me to hunt and kill while you make fire?'

He grinned. 'Be my guest. Go bash a barley sugar to death.'

'I'm far too sensitive. They look at me with their big brown eyes.' Then she saw his hands and her smile died. 'You need to let me help. Your hands are already blistering with sunburn.'

'Yours are prettier than mine to start with,' he said. 'Why spoil four hands? But you might usefully hunt and kill firewood. Does driftwood look at you?'

So that was what she did, keeping a watchful eye for the ospreys. And crocodiles. She had to clamber down too close for comfort to the croc-threatening waterline. That made Finn nervous as well, but they both knew they had no choice. The wood was below the high tide mark.

'Just get down and back fast,' he told her. A flag during the day and fires at night were their best chance—their only chance—of attracting the attention of rescuers.

She worked on, diving in and out of the shade, climbing down and up from the waterline. Finally she'd collected a pile big enough for a decent nightlong blaze. She headed back to Finn— and he was staring at a flame with awe.

'I feel like I've just passed Basic Boy Scout Training,' he breathed, and he looked like a kid on Christmas morning. He looked…adorable, she thought. Before she could think it through, she knelt beside him and hugged him.

Then she pulled away and inspected his fire— and inspected him. She wanted to hug him again. Sense prevailed.

'Your poor hands…' she managed. 'Let's get some water on them.'

'And your nose is bright red,' he said. 'Water on that as well?'

The fierceness was finally going out of the sun. They headed back to their waterhole, cupped their hands and drank, allowing a little for sunburned noses.

'We'll move to rationing when it gets half full,' Finn decreed. 'But for now…'

For now they had to face the night with water and dwindling barley sugar. It wasn't enough to keep hunger at bay. It wasn't enough to keep fear at bay.

'Tomorrow we try roasting lizards?' Rachel said doubtfully.

'Maybe we could raid the ospreys' nest. If the eggs have only just been laid we could have osprey omelette.'

'Ugh,' she said. 'You get to climb and steal them. Good luck.' She hesitated, eyeing another barley sugar. 'I wonder what they're having on the ship right now.'

'Nothing,' Finn said promptly. 'They'll be sitting round in mourning clothes, not eating out of respect. Sobbing into their empty plates while they keep a lookout in case we happen to drift past.'

'They won't return to look for us?' It was almost wistful.

'They can't,' Finn said gently. 'The Captain's responsibility is to all of his passengers. These are uncharted waters with huge tides. There's no way he can turn and search. He'll leave it to others.'

'Just as well we have Maud, then,' she whispered and he watched her face and he thought, *Please, Maud...*

They were depending on an eighty-three-year-old woman. On a woman who loved Rachel.

They were depending on a love he was just barely starting to understand.

As darkness fell they lit fires on the three points of the island so searchers could see them from any direction.

'I'll stoke them during the night,' Finn decreed. 'I'll keep them flaming. Tomorrow we'll let them smoulder. The trails of smoke will be seen for miles.'

'But you're sure…' She didn't finish, but he knew what she was asking.

'That only the right people will be searching? I'm sure.' He met her gaze directly, glad he could believe what he was telling her. 'Wasting manpower trying to find us is not what drug runners do.'

'I can't believe anyone could be so wicked.'

They'd settled back on the same ledge where they'd slept the night before. The afternoon sun had warmed the sand underneath, giving as much comfort as they could hope for, but for now, Rachel wasn't comforted. Darkness had brought the return of demons. He heard the shake in her voice and he tugged her close.

For a moment he felt her resist.

'We need to hold,' he said gently. 'I'm as scared as you.'

She tugged away from him a little at that, and gazed at him in the moonlight. This time he did see disbelief. 'You are not,' she said. 'You're a Boy Scout. Boy Scouts are prepared—not scared.'

'If I was prepared I'd have brought a condom,' he said mournfully, and she gasped—and then choked on laughter, which was just the reaction he wanted.

'Dream on,' she said. 'Condoms or not, that scenario is definitely in your dreams. You should only prepare for possibilities.'

'Or hopes?' He sounded...hopeful.

'Not even that.' Her smile deepened. Strangely, the mention of an absent condom seemed to have broken the ice.

'You really were a Scout?' she asked.

'A Cub,' he told her. 'I didn't get to the big boy stuff.' By the time he'd reached the age for Scouts he already had a part-time job and there was little time for pleasure. His mother was dead and his grandparents were struggling. His grandfather had found him a job in the shipyard and he'd learned more on the job than he ever would at Scouts.

'Where were you raised?' she asked, and he tugged her close again because it seemed the most natural thing to do. She hesitated, but then she obviously decided not to be dumb, to take what both of them needed. She curved against him, her back to his chest, spooning to gain maximum warmth.

Maximum comfort.

But, for him, there was more…

He could feel every inch of her body under the flimsy nightdress. A lesser man…

He wasn't a lesser man—and he didn't have a condom.

The world seemed all wrong. What seemed right was taking this woman to him, right here, right now.

It was not going to happen.

What had she asked? It was impossible to concentrate on words when she was just… She was just…

Concentrate. Where had he been raised?

'Maine,' he managed. 'On the East Coast of the US.'

'Tell me about it.'

'What would you like to know?'

'Anything you want to tell me,' she said, as if he was dumb. 'I've never left Australia. How big is it? Did you live near the sea?'

These were commonplace questions. He forced himself to relax. He held her close and her warmth made him feel as if his defences were crumbling.

Defences?

He did have defences, he thought. Maybe he always had. He rarely talked about his background. Why should he?

But then he thought about Maine and the childhood he'd loved, and he thought he could go there.

'My grandfather was a boat-builder, so we lived by the sea,' he said. 'There wasn't anything Pop couldn't do with his hands, and when he wasn't building boats he was sailing them. That was my life. He taught me all he could and then he found me an apprenticeship with the best wooden boat-builder he knew. He had a yacht he'd built himself—wood, of course, and he took me sailing from the time I first remember. I was his shadow. His shipmate, he called me.'

'He sounds lovely.'

'He was.'

'He's dead?' she asked hesitantly, and he figured that was another question he could answer. Talking was what Rachel needed. Maybe talking was what they both needed.

'My mom was born late,' he told her. 'She was the child my grandparents never dared to hope they'd have. They adored her, but when she died Gran fell apart. Gran died when I was fifteen and Pop died soon after.'

'Did you get to know your dad's parents?'

Whoa. Stop now, he thought. There's no need to go on. There's no need to tell her more.

But, strangely, his need to talk was stronger than his customary need for reserve. And Rachel wasn't a stranger. Rachel was the woman he was holding in his arms.

'No,' he said bluntly. 'I didn't even meet my dad. He never wanted to meet me.'

'I never knew my dad, either,' she told him. 'Maybe he's still alive.'

'Mine's definitely dead.'

'Is that good?' she asked cautiously, and he found himself smiling. The way she'd asked... As if the question might bite but she was going there anyway.

She was asking him to open up—as she'd just opened up.

'I guess it is,' he admitted. 'He didn't treat my mom very well.'

'Want to tell me about it?'

This was an extraordinary conversation. It

was a conversation he'd never had with anyone. Until now.

'My mom's health was always fragile,' he said. 'When she was nineteen, influenza turned into pneumonia. She took ages to recover; and, when she was finally on her feet, Gran and Pop sent her on a cruise to the tropics. It was mid-winter in Maine and the doctor told them it'd do her good. Only, of course, there was no money for them to go with her. So off she went, half silly with the excitement of it, scared of being alone but determined to enjoy herself. And of course vulnerable is too small a word to describe how she must have appeared to my father. She came back pregnant, and of course my father didn't want to know. They hadn't invented DNA testing then. Not that Mom or my grandparents would have wanted it. They just got on with the job of raising me as best they could.'

Silence. And then…disbelief? But not of the story he'd just told. Her look in the moonlight was much more searching, as if she was trying to connect the dots and they weren't in the same dimension.

And suddenly he realised what she was thinking. 'So now you have two kids conceived the same way?' She tugged back and stared accusingly down at him in the dim light. 'I don't believe you.'

Whoa, that was a mistake. What to do? Tell her the truth?

He could, but that'd lead to more questions. Maybe it needed to stop now.

'Believe what you want,' he said softly.

There was a long silence then, and her gaze turned thoughtful. Intelligent. And, finally, she looked as if she knew the answer. 'You told Maud that to scare her off,' she said slowly. 'Because of the matchmaking. There are no kids.'

'There are kids, Rachel.'

'What are their names?'

'Connie and Richard.'

She glowered. 'I don't like guys who lie to me.'

'You don't have to like me.'

'Are you kidding? How about that whole condom conversation?'

'Is having sex liking?'

That produced another silence. That had been a blunt question. A cruel question. A question to drive her away.

Like he'd driven women away in the past.

This was crazy. It had been an instinctive reaction to her probing. An instinctive defence. He didn't need to drive her away. He didn't even want to.

Did he?

But maybe he hadn't. She was still watching him, calmly assessing. Instead of retreating, her gaze was asking more questions.

He was starting to feel exposed, as if she could see into places he'd long kept hidden. The feeling was...disconcerting. 'What were you doing with your phone camera back on the ship?' she demanded suddenly, and he stilled. It was as if she'd discovered one lie and was looking for more.

'Taking photographs of drug runners,' he admitted.

'You were expecting them to be there?'

'I...yes.' She'd work that out. He might as well be as honest as he could. 'I heard the ship stop and knew it wasn't supposed to. It stopped a couple of nights before as well, so I thought I'd investigate.'

She was still staring at him, trying to work

him out. 'Who are you?' she demanded, her eyes never leaving his face.

'Me,' he said simply. 'Finn Kinnard.'

'Not a cop? But not a boat-builder either. Investigator?'

'Of a sort.'

'For heaven's sake,' she said, exasperated. 'Why the secrecy? Are you one of those secret service guys with false moustaches and security clearances that make ordinary people's eyes water?'

'Um…no,' he said and grinned. 'Not a single moustache.'

'But there's something,' she said shrewdly. 'I think…'

'You don't need to think,' he said gently. 'We both know there's more behind everyone's façade than meets the eye. As far as I can, I'm telling you the truth.'

'But there is more?'

'There is,' he agreed. 'Like you. There's so much I don't know about your life. What about letting your barriers down?'

'Like…'

'Like telling me about your baby,' he said gently. 'Like telling me what broke your heart.'

CHAPTER EIGHT

FOR a long while Finn thought Rachel wouldn't answer. She stayed staring at him in the dim light, as if she was trying to figure him out. Whatever conclusion she came to, it obviously wasn't cut and run. Finally she sighed and lay down again. He put his arms around her and tugged her close.

She lay stiff for a while, but finally he felt her relax.

'You're not being honest with me,' she said.

'Why should I be honest with you?'

'You don't need to tell me,' he said softly into the night. 'I'm just trying to distract us from lack of barley sugar.'

'Tomorrow morning's breakfast is roast lizard,' she said, and he felt her body relax even more. Good. They both needed contact, the feeling that they weren't alone. They also needed food. A breakfast of lizard was something they could laugh about, even if the laughter was kind of hollow. He really was hungry.

'Do we know how to cook roast lizard?' he asked.

'We could check it out on the Internet,' she suggested. 'If you have an Internet connection on your Boy Scout's knife. Or we could use the method my grandma taught me.'

'Your grandma taught you how to cook lizard?'

He heard her smile, and their bodies moved infinitesimally closer.

'In theory. We never got to practise. There was a dearth of lizards in the apartments where we lived. Come to think of it, there was a dearth of campfires, too.'

He lay and held her and let the thought drift. A grandmother teaching a child how to cook lizard…

She'd told him her grandma was Koori. Rachel wasn't all Koori but the best parts of her must surely be. The lovely dusky skin. The gorgeous dark eyes…

'Your grandma was a lizard cooker?'

'Extraordinaire,' Rachel said and chuckled.

'And fire maker. If she were here she wouldn't have needed a sissy knife.'

'Hey!'

'Sorry,' she said, and she chuckled again and nestled closer. The laughter died. The silence grew deeper. 'You really want to hear about my baby?' she asked into the stillness, and his breath caught in his throat.

He was being offered something, he thought. Why did it feel like…a gift without price?

He should say now. He didn't get that kind of close. He'd only asked to divert her, but now…

He did want to know. He badly wanted to know. 'If you want to tell me,' he said, and waited.

'I sort of do,' she confessed. 'I don't talk about her very often but… If I talk about her, somehow she's real. She *is* real. I don't want her to be gone for everyone except me.'

'So tell me about her,' he said softly, and she heard the sincerity in his voice.

So he held her close and listened, while she talked about falling for the principal dancer in the company her sister belonged to, about emerging from the academic world she lived in to become a lovesick kid who couldn't see past the fact that this gorgeous male dancer wanted her. She talked about a marriage—brief, fiery—and a guy's temper that made her afraid.

He held her while she talked about the times when the company was in recess and Ramón wasn't dancing—and the drinking and the escalating violence.

He held her while she talked about a night, a car, a crash—and waking to find her daughter being born. Named Elizabeth after Rachel's grandmother. Twenty-eight weeks' gestation, and battered, too small to survive.

'I was awake enough to hold her,' she whispered. 'I remember her breathing. I remember her tiny finger curled around mine. For that short time I had her and I held her, and she's in my heart for ever. I'd been injured but I can't remember hurting. I can't remember anything but my baby, and I'll always be thankful to the doctors for holding off treating my injuries until my baby girl no longer needed me.'

She fell silent. She lay cocooned against him, and he didn't know what she was thinking.

Or maybe he did. One tiny girl who might have lived.

And what this Ramón had done—it made him seethe.

He knew he wanted to do violence to something, someone, for letting this woman suffer.

He knew he wanted to hold her until...until...

He couldn't go past that thought.

He held her. After a while she slept and still he held her.

The fires needed stoking. He didn't know how to let her go.

He didn't know how to want to.

'I'm glad you're here,' she murmured as she drifted to sleep, and he thought, *So am I.*

Why was he keeping his defences against her?

He couldn't, not for much longer.

He needed to keep the fires burning. Intermittently during the night he had to disengage himself and leave her. She murmured a protest in her sleep. She tried to hold and he kissed her—because it seemed natural and right and it seemed to give her reassurance—and then he made his way around their tiny island to stoke up their beacons.

Rachel had heaped huge loads of fuel beside each fire site. While he'd struggled with making the fire itself, she'd clambered down and up, down and up the shale cliff, collecting generations of driftwood caught among the rocks on the shoreline.

He'd hated her doing it. Okay, the risk of crocodile attack was tiny. Crocs were creatures of habit, and habit wouldn't have them hunting here. But they'd use these low-lying rocks to rest or to devour their prey. There'd been a risk.

It had taken him hours to get the fire alight—as the raw skin on his hands still told. He'd had to do it. Rachel had needed to gather firewood—there'd been no choice about that either—but she'd done it with no complaint and she'd collected more than he could possibly have expected.

She had an injured hip. She'd climbed up and down most of the day. No wonder she was sleeping now.

How much must she be hurting?

He thought of her as he stoked the fires, and

he kept on thinking. His body was still achingly aware of her, even though he was on the far side of the island.

Something was twisting inside him, something deep and primeval, and he didn't understand it. He didn't know what to do about it.

When he'd first seen this woman he'd reacted with distrust. Little, cute, vulnerable. Like his mother and grandmother. Like all his father's 'victims'.

But there was nothing victim-like about Rachel. She was a geologist with an injured hip and a grief that was heart-deep. She was a woman who made him smile. She was a woman who made his body burn.

He should have told her all the truth, he thought. She didn't believe he had children. She knew he'd said it to make Maud lose interest.

He'd explain the kids.

But the rest? That he owned this cruise line?

Maybe not yet.

And maybe that was because he wasn't sure of the way he was feeling. He didn't understand it—all he knew was that he didn't want anything to mess with it.

And money did mess with relationships. He'd seen that over and over, since he'd inherited his father's fortune.

When his father died he'd been dating a girl who lived next door to his grandfather—dating in a light-hearted way. They'd been friends more than lovers.

But the moment she'd heard about his inheritance she was deathly serious, hysterically excited, clinging. She'd always assumed they'd marry, she told him. Of course she had.

And when he'd backed away, saying, 'Slow down, I'm not sure,' she'd threatened to sue.

The way she'd reacted to his money appalled him. It made him wary of telling anyone he was more than a boat-builder—he didn't now, unless he had no choice. He didn't much like his new persona as wealthy shipping magnate, and he didn't like the way women reacted to it.

This wasn't the first time he'd used his half-brother and sister as a shield. *'I'm already caring for kids. I'm not in the market for a relationship.'*

He'd carefully reinforced his armour. He'd decided he was destined for bachelorhood.

So now... Was he prepared to shed the armour

he'd so carefully constructed? After knowing Rachel for less than a week?

The logical part of him said it didn't make sense—but the logic wasn't operating right now.

It must be trauma that was making him feel like this, he decided, as he stacked logs onto the fires. It was adrenalin rather than hormones. Nothing else explained it.

It wasn't sensible—but something inside him was saying sense didn't come into it. What was front and foremost was that Rachel was unlike any woman he'd ever met.

She made him feel different. She made him want to believe.

In what? In happy ever after? In rainbows and nightingales and confetti?

He straightened from loading the largest of Rachel's logs onto the fire—*how had she dragged this up the cliff?*—and managed a wry smile.

Was the way he was feeling caused by adrenalin?

Or not.

He wanted it to be not.

'Is that why you're not telling her you own the cruise line? Are you afraid of how she'll react?

Are you afraid the illusion will shatter and she'll be just like the others?' He asked the questions out loud.

No one answered. Of course they didn't. Two nights on a deserted island and he was already losing his mind.

'Get a grip,' he told himself. 'You need to keep a plan in place. Be logical.

'And lie to the lady?

'It's not lying, simply not telling her I own the cruise line. I don't want to see her face change.

'It won't change.'

It might. He knew by now that wealth scared as well as attracted.

'There's too much emotion here already,' he told the leaping flames. 'Too many complications. Get off this island before you make any decisions.'

That was sensible and a man had to be sensible.

He also had to go back to Rachel.

They woke in the pre-dawn light and headed for their waterhole. The level was starting to fall, despite Rachel's jacket.

There was nothing more they could do to protect it.

They moved to another ledge, in the shade. By mutual consent, they ate two more pieces of barley sugar. They had eight pieces left.

There was nothing left to do. They went back to lying side by side, just touching, looking out over the ocean.

It was the most comfortable position, Finn thought. It was sensible—conserving energy, taking and giving comfort.

Waiting.

And talking?

'Tell me about the kids,' she asked into the stillness and he realised they hadn't talked for half an hour. This woman was…restful.

Special.

'What do you want to know?'

'Are they yours?'

And there was something in her voice that said *Don't lie.*

So he didn't. 'They're my father's,' he told her. 'They're younger than me, but they're my half siblings.'

She considered for a while, thoughtful rather than reactive.

'Maud will be pleased,' she said at last.

'That's what I'm afraid of,' he said, and he felt her smile. And then go back to thinking.

'Their mother can't take care of them?'

He thought of Richard and Connie as he'd last seen them. Then he thought of how he'd first met them.

'They have different mothers,' he said.

'And you're supporting them?'

'They live with me, but my father left enough to pay for their keep,' he said curtly. There was no reason to take that further, either, to tell her how the money had been left, or how much money they were talking about.

But she was figuring things out for herself. She was figuring him out. She wriggled and turned so she was facing him.

'Where are they now?'

'At home. We have a housekeeper. A good one.'

'Then you're not just a boat-builder,' she said, and it wasn't a question. 'There are lots of things you're not telling me, Mr Mysterious. This drug thing… It's not accidental that you were up there watching.'

'No.' He didn't have a choice—she already knew.

'And you'd rather not tell me why?'

'I…yes.'

She gazed at him for a long time and then gave a decisive nod.

'I can live with that,' she said. 'I've decided you're an undercover cop, travelling the world rooting out evil. Under that bronzed chest you're wearing skin-tight Lycra emblazoned with a huge S for Superhero. If a croc appears you'll disappear into your phone booth, shed your skin, emerge in your leotard and carry me skywards.'

He chuckled but shook his head. 'I've seen the wood you lugged up the cliff. If there's any S, it's under your nightdress.'

'You'd know,' she said and grinned and he smiled at her and she smiled back—and suddenly the need to kiss her was overwhelming. Totally, absolutely overwhelming.

And he looked at her and he knew she was thinking exactly the same thing.

'Tell me about the boats you've built,' she said hastily—too hastily. Suddenly sounding panicky.

'My boats equate to your rocks,' he told her. 'I'm passionate. You don't want to get me started.'

'Don't I?'

'No.'

'Hmm.' She leaned forward and took his hands in hers, studying them as if reading life lines.

'You *are* a boat-builder,' she said thoughtfully. 'Or you were. These hands have been battered, but not for a while. You're getting soft.'

'Hey!'

'No offence,' she said and smiled. 'The blisters you got yesterday make up for it.'

'Rachel…'

'And the blisters you'll get today,' she decreed. 'You're on wood-fetching duty this morning. I'll look after the fires.'

'Yes, ma'am,' he said, and thought there were things he wanted to do more than cart wood.

Much more.

But they were trapped on this island. This situation was fraught.

And… He didn't have a condom.

She'd described him as honourable.

The way she was looking at him, it was a very hard descriptor to live up to.

The morning passed slowly. Too slowly, considering the amount of barley sugar they had left. And water.

They made their fires smoulder rather than flame, using damp wood rather than dry stuff, and then turned their attention to hunting.

'We need a waddy,' Rachel decreed.

'What's a waddy?'

'Grandma had one. She called it her *amirre*, a mix of spear and club. She kept it in the wardrobe in case of burglars. I'm not sure where it's gone—when we went into foster care we couldn't take it with us.' She chuckled. 'Can you imagine— "Will you take care of these two cute little girls? And, by the way, they have a waddy and they know how to use it."'

'I can't imagine,' he said faintly. 'So, without a waddy…'

'We're in trouble.' Her smile faded and she stared out at the horizon.

'They'll come,' she said. Humour aside, this

place was inaccessible, uncharted, a thousand miles from anywhere. 'And your family... Won't they be looking?'

His family. Connie and Richard? They'd be distressed to know he'd gone missing but it wouldn't change things. When they'd first come to live with him they'd seemed distant, almost scared of him, but gradually they'd started letting him act like the big brother he was. He worried about them. He'd spent time with them, getting them the help they needed to start on careers they enjoyed. He even put up with their appalling tastes in music. He knew he'd grown fond of the two of them, but they'd been on their own for so long that they'd learned not to need. His loss surely wouldn't leave a hole in their lives.

And, as if she sensed the thought, Rachel moved imperceptibly closer and hugged him.

'Don't worry,' she said softly. 'You can share Maud. You can have the matchmaking part.'

'Wow, thanks.'

She chuckled. The wobble had gone again.

How could she keep smiling? Her nightdress was ripped, her hair was matted and her nose was sunburned and blistered. She must be as hungry as he was and, no matter how much she trusted Maud, she must know how precarious their position was.

But her smile was pinned firmly back in place.

'You could do with a matchmaker,' she said. 'When we get back I'll tell Maud to do her worst. One honourable scoundrel, in need of a good woman to take care of him and his siblings. I don't know what you are, Finn Kinnard, but I do know you mean well.'

'Um… Thank you.'

'Mind, I'm a hopeless judge of character. I shouldn't trust you at all.'

'You can trust me,' he said.

'I think I can,' she said thoughtfully. 'You don't lie. Not directly. I'm figuring that out. But I wish you could be honest.'

Tell her. Now.

Why not?

A lizard darted from under the rocks, right at their feet, and Rachel grabbed—and missed.

'I need my waddy,' she said.

'I don't think this island runs to a waddy shop.'

'That's where you come in, my superhero with

Boy Scout penknife,' she decreed. 'I'll draw a construction diagram in the sand, and you do the rest. That's what superheroes do.'

'Really?'

'Really,' she said and smiled in a way that twisted his heart like it had never been twisted.

It was the place, the isolation, the shared fear, he told himself. It must be.

But as he watched her clamber over the rocks in search of suitable wood for her waddy—he should help and in a moment he would but for now, for this instant, he just watched—he knew it was far more than that.

Far more.

Something was breaking inside him. Some armour he'd never thought could be pierced.

This woman…

If she asked more, he'd tell her.

'Oi,' she yelled back at him. 'Sharpen your knife while you're waiting, Superhero.'

'Yes, ma'am,' he called back faintly. 'Anything you say.'

They built an awesome waddy. It took them two hours, which was two hours where they could concentrate on something other than how hungry they were—and then a helicopter came in from the south.

It was a dot at first, weaving between distant islands—and then someone on board must have seen the smoke because it changed direction and came in low and fast, not deviating, heading straight for them.

Rescue? Or…

'Do you suppose…?' He glanced at Rachel and saw the colour had drained from her face.

'Do you think…?' she whispered.

He put his arm around her and held. Tight. 'That this is the good guys?' he asked. 'Yes, I do.' He said it firmly, definitely, and he held her hard and he tried to believe it.

He did believe it. It made sense.

'It's red,' Rachel said, shading her face and staring as if she was willing field glasses into her hand. 'Amy says Hugo flies a red chopper.'

'Hugo?'

'My soon-to-be brother-in-law.'

What were the chances of her sister's fiancé finding them? It'd be Search and Rescue, or even the army if Maud had that sort of pull, Finn thought—but the chopper was definitely red and it was zeroing in.

'Should…should we wave?' Rachel's voice was tremulous and he pulled her closer still.

'We don't have a choice,' he said firmly. 'If we hide we don't get rescued, and even roast lizard might get boring. Plus I left my razor behind. So if you don't want to be castaway with The Old Man of The Sea…'

'H…heaven forbid.'

'Then we wave.'

They did, stepping out into the sunshine and waving like lunatics.

And then the chopper was right over them, swooping so low they could see a figure frantically waving back from the passenger seat. Beside them was the pilot, intent on his controls, but as they made their first sweep he raised his hand as well.

'It's Amy.' Rachel was waving and sobbing, waving and sobbing, hardly coherent through her sobs. 'It's my Amy and her Hugo. It's my family. I knew they'd come.'

And as Finn watched the wild waving from above he thought…

Her family.

She had people who loved her and were claiming her.

Here was rescue. He should be jubilant—and part of him was. But why was he feeling as if he was losing something?

It was something he never had, he told himself fiercely.

He could have it.

Don't go there, he told himself harshly. Or not yet. This was too precious, too amazing to rush.

One step at a time.

But still he was faced with the sense that he was losing her.

'It seems a shame to waste the waddy,' he managed. 'You want to tell them to come back tomorrow?'

'The waddy gets rescued as well,' Rachel said, smiling and smiling. 'And the lizard population will be grateful to see it go. I intend to use my waddy on beef steak instead. Mmm, beef steak. And chips. And maybe a dollop of ice cream on the side. You want to join me? I think our ride's waiting.'

CHAPTER NINE

AMY and Hugo circled the tiny island half a dozen times so there could be no doubt that Finn and Rachel knew they were indeed found, but there was little they could do about rescuing them. They dropped a padded box of water bottles and biscuits and dried fruit—which shattered on the rocks, but enough remained intact to protect the lizard population. They waved fiercely again, signalling more help was on the way, then zoomed off in their little red chopper back to the mainland.

'Their machine has a limited range,' Finn told Rachel as she watched them leave in dismay. 'It's a miracle they found us—their refuelling base will be miles inland. But the big guns will come now.'

And the big guns did come—two army choppers, fast, powerful, purposeful.

Two minutes after they arrived, a guy in rescue gear was winched down to join them.

'Boy, are we pleased to see you,' the uniformed paramedic said. 'Any injuries?'

'Sunburn, ant bites, sore feet and blisters,' Finn managed. 'Nothing to worry about at all. And you're not as pleased to see us as we are to see you.'

'You have one old lady to thank for that,' he told them. 'Plus the Thurston empire. We couldn't have searched without the resources Dame Maud's commandeered, not when the *Temptress* Captain told us you must be dead. The crew was certain. They'll be over the moon to know you're found.'

'Can you stop them knowing?' Finn asked.

The guy was looking at Finn's hands. Assessing damage. He paused and raised a brow in question.

'I need to get a message to the police, urgently,' Finn said. 'We're fine, but we didn't fall from the *Temptress*.'

'Word is that you guys were having a midnight tryst,' the man said mildly, but he'd seen the way Finn had tugged Rachel close and the way Rachel clung. 'Word is that you got carried away on a rough night, and toppled right in. So…no tryst?'

'The tryst wasn't of our making.'

'You're trysting now,' the guy pointed out, grinning. He'd grinned since he'd reached them. Finn guessed not many of this guy's searches resulted in happy endings.

'We've learned how to tryst,' Rachel said, smiling back at him. Smiling and smiling. 'Trysting's an important survival technique. Finn, can't we tell Maud?'

'Is Dame Maud still on the *Temptress*?'

'As far as I know,' the guy said, 'the cruise has continued. We offered to take her off but she told us all resources were to be used to look for you.'

'There's a drug cache on that boat,' Finn said evenly. 'That's why we were forced overboard. If we've had to spend all this time…trysting…I want to be sure someone pays.'

'Trysting's that bad, huh?' The man was working fast. He was already edging Rachel away from Finn, fitting a harness ready to winch her off the island.

'It's not so bad,' Finn admitted, looking at Rachel—who blushed and looked back at him. Directly, meeting his gaze and smiling even more. Making his heart do that crazy twisting thing he was starting to get to know. Starting to like.

'It's had its moments,' she agreed. 'A couple of them weren't too bad.'

Then she chuckled and she turned her attention to the harness—and Finn watched her being winched skyward and thought, *Where do we go from here?*

Back to reality.

Which was?

Back to the principles he'd followed all his adult life?

Maybe not.

Maybe things had changed for ever.

They were taken to a mining camp fifty miles inland, the closest place for refuelling, a barren, dusty camp in the middle of nowhere. One little red helicopter was waiting for them, and a woman who looked very like Rachel, who sobbed and sobbed and held her sister so tight Finn thought they might fuse.

The rescue personnel held back, giving them

space. The pilot of the red chopper—introduced hastily by an overwrought Rachel as Hugo Thurston—gripped Finn's hand and watched the women, and Finn thought this guy looked like he'd seen tough things before and he was soaking up what had just happened.

'I couldn't see this ending up good,' he said gruffly. 'And for us to find you... We figured we'd do the edges, the perimeter of the search range the big guys might miss. But how the hell did you get there? The tidal patterns...the currents...'

'The ship was way off course.'

'Which explains why you want to talk to the cops before we relay any message that you're safe and well?' Rachel's future brother-in-law was sharp, Finn thought. As head of Thurston Holdings, he'd have to be.

Some time during the long hours Rachel had told him about Hugo. This was Dame Maud's grandson, heir to the Thurston empire, but before he'd joined the family firm he'd trained and worked for years as a commando. It showed.

'If I find you dragged her into this...' Hugo

said quite pleasantly, almost as if it were idle chat. 'If I find you have one tiny finger in any drug-running pie...'

'Hey, I'm the good guy here,' Finn said, but part of him thought that maybe Hugo had grounds for accusation. He'd suspected drug-running. Why hadn't he done more?

But then, how could he sack a whole crew because of the suspicion that it contained a couple of criminals? It was contrary to every workplace law he knew. And he was only working on suspicions. He had to have proof.

Finding that proof had almost killed Rachel, but it wasn't his fault.

'I wouldn't hurt her for the world,' he said, almost inconsequentially, and Hugo glanced at him and his face changed. Maybe something in Finn's voice had revealed more than he wanted to reveal.

'They do that to you,' Hugo said softly, and he turned back to watch the hugging women. 'The Cotton sisters. They're capable of changing a man's life, and you have the look of a man whose life is changing already. Welcome to the club, mate—and good luck.'

* * *

Things moved fast. Finn's story pushed buttons in high places. They were in one of the most remote places in Australia, but within two hours they were joined by senior police and customs officers—men and women who looked like they meant business and knew how to go about it.

'We've had drugs flooding the country through the northern ports,' the senior customs official explained. 'If this is as big as we think it is…'

Rachel and Amy had headed off to the camp's shower block with a warning they might be some time. Finn was hunkered down with the officials—and so was Hugo, staying in the background, watching and listening. It seemed Hugo knew some of these guys. He wasn't leaving.

The first few minutes Finn spent explaining who he was. Hugo's expression changed when he heard, but he said nothing. He kept on listening.

Someone had a universal charger for Finn's phone. They got the photos up, put them on a computer, enlarged them, and the custom guy's expression changed from straight grim to satisfied grim. His was a look that said Esme was going to regret this for a long, long time.

'We'll get a *swat* team together, send a couple of our big choppers out and take them by surprise before they have a chance to dump the drugs,' the chief told Finn. 'You guys are listed as an accident. They've had no reason to toss the drugs overboard when no one's given any hint we think you've survived. If we go in fast and hard, we'll pick up these three and the Captain—he must have known. There are probably more involved but we can sort that back in port. We'll turn the ship back to Darwin, get statements, go from there.'

'Why not let it keep going?' Finn suggested. 'The cruise line has contingencies for replacing staff mid-cruise. We get rid of those we know are rotten, and it's business as normal.'

'There'll be more…'

'That's what I mean,' Finn said gently. 'I'd like to go back on board, stay as a passenger and keep my ear to the ground.'

'We need to take Maud off,' Hugo said from behind them and Finn turned and met Hugo's hard gaze.

'If she wishes, then of course she can leave. But I've met the lady. Will she wish?'

'If she stays, Rachel will want to return, and I won't have them risk…'

'You seriously think there's continued risk?'

There was a moment's silence while everyone assessed what was being proposed. Four criminals removed from the boat, and the cruise would continue as usual.

'There's no reason why not,' Finn said.

'Does Rachel know you're the undercover boss of the whole cruise line?' Hugo demanded.

'No,' Finn said evenly. 'And if she comes back on board, I'd prefer her not to know.'

'Why?'

'How good's her acting? And Maud's? Could they treat me as a normal passenger? That's what I still am—a normal passenger who's been the victim of a crime. If anyone else on board figures who I am, why I'm there, it'll make my presence useless. But there's no Internet, and the new Captain can control radio access. Would it hurt to leave me undercover until Broome? Rachel thinks I'm some sort of security agent but she doesn't know for sure. I won't be asking her to act a part. I don't want to ask any more of her than she's already given.'

There was another pause. A long one.

'I can see your point,' Hugo said at last. 'But I'm not sure I like it. Not to tell them the truth...'

'I will, as soon as we get to Broome.'

'You want them to calmly continue their cruise?'

'I suspect they might like to. They deserve a holiday. Telling them who I am and asking them to keep it secret...it's a pressure they don't need.'

And...how to explain that he wanted it, too. Badly. He wanted a few more days of normal, when he could get to know Rachel as he wanted to. Explore the way he was feeling. See if he could figure where to go from here.

His life wasn't normal. He'd never expected to inherit his father's fortune—or Connie and Richard. More, he'd never expected to feel the way he was feeling about any woman. Now... To ask Rachel to be part of what he was barely accepting himself...

He wasn't even sure whether he wanted to. All he knew was that he needed time. Time when Rachel thought *he* was almost normal.

And, overriding everything else, was his concern for her. During the long nights on the island he'd realised she lived with nightmares. She'd stirred in the night, sobbing, confused, mixing car smashes and the death of her baby and the nightmare in the sea.

Maybe the way to keep nightmares at bay was to give her back the cruise she'd dreamed of. Give her things to dream about that weren't horrific.

'One hint of trouble...' Hugo growled.

'I'll stay in contact with the police every step of the way,' he assured him. 'But we all know anyone still on board with drug connections will keep their heads down.'

'And you'll leave her alone until she knows who you are?'

'What are you, her guardian?'

'I'm marrying her sister,' Hugo growled. 'You've brought her trouble and I don't like it. I don't like deceiving her and I'm thinking I'd like you to keep away from her until it's over.'

He had to be kidding.

His hard glare said he wasn't.

Keep away from her?

He should do his best to keep things slow between them, he conceded. It was only fair. But after Broome…

After Broome they'd be just two normal people.

Normal people fell in love.

She was returning from her shower, walking back to him with Amy. She was dressed in oversized khaki shorts and a shirt one of the men had found for her. Her curls were dripping wetly down her back and he thought… He thought…

He thought, like it or not, he already had.

'You're playing with fire, not telling her,' Hugo growled. 'Don't underestimate her intelligence. Or her reaction if she thinks she's been lied to.'

'I'm not lying.'

'You're not telling her the truth. Same thing.'

And out at sea…

A couple of powerful choppers arrived without warning over the anchored *Kimberley Temptress*. Swat guys, armed and dangerous and skilled, dropped onto the ship before the crew or passengers could react.

The search for drugs, the arrest and removal of the four crew members, shocked the passengers to numbness, but any dismay and distress they might feel was tempered with the news that Finn and Rachel had been found.

It'd give his customers a cruise to talk about all their lives, Finn thought, imagining home movies of the magnificent Kimberley—and swat teams swarming the decks of a cruise ship, armed for hand to hand combat.

There'd been no resistance. Esme and her lot knew when they were beaten. Already Finn had crew members flying from Darwin to take their places.

When he and Rachel rejoined the cruise they'd be treated as heroes, he thought. With the resultant publicity… It might even end up being good for business.

That wasn't why he was going back.

He was returning to see if anyone else on board was corrupt—but there was another reason.

He was returning because he wanted normal. He wanted a few days when they could be singles on board with nothing to do but enjoy their holiday. He wanted time without his wealth or position interfering with how she felt—changing things, making her reassess once again. He

wanted time with nothing to do but see if he
could do something about Rachel's nightmares.

Nothing to do but fall in love?

'It makes sense. We've paid for this holiday,'
he told her as they waited for the chopper to take
them back, for Rachel seemed as keen to return
as he was.

'Maud paid for me and I don't believe you paid
at all.'

'No?'

'I think you're an undercover security guy for
the cruise line. Nothing else makes sense. Your
job is to be on the *Kimberley Temptress*, looking for trouble. Yes or no?'

He hesitated. Thinking how not to deepen the
lie.

'Not just the *Kimberley Temptress*,' he admitted. 'I'm responsible for the security of the whole
Temptress line.'

'I knew it!'

'Well guessed. But please keep it to yourself.'

'Does Hugo know?'

'Yes.'

'Then Amy will, too,' she said with satisfaction. 'They'll know I'm not messing with a phi-landerer.'

'Are we...messing?'

'I'm not sure,' she admitted, surprisingly. 'Two days ago I'd have said no, but now...you make me feel...' She broke off. 'Enough. This emotion's all mixed up with what's happened—the pressure, the fear. It's far too soon to figure... what I really feel.'

'It's much too soon,' he agreed, thinking this was all about taking the pressure off, but his gaze didn't break from hers and he watched her blush and he thought... You are the most beautiful woman in the world. Bar none. No question.

Too soon. Keep it in mind. Keep it strongly in mind.

'I have a question,' she said. 'A biggie.'

'Which is?'

'The kids...' she said, surprising him.

'Connie and Richard?'

'Yes. Do you love them?'

The question was as unexpected as it was hard to answer. He had to wait. He had to think.

He thought of Connie and Richard as he'd found them. He thought of how he'd felt, discovering his own father had put them in that mess. Anger didn't begin to describe it. He thought of what they'd done since then. He thought of what they were becoming. Kids, shaking off adversity and finding a future. He was proud of them, he conceded, but he kept his pride to himself. They were prickly, aloof, and they didn't do emotion.

'Why ask?' he said, prevaricating.

'Because it worries me,' she said. 'To be on the other side of the world, doing something so dangerous…'

'I never, ever intended that my life be at risk on this journey,' he said, gently now, accepting her worry.

'So you do love them?'

'I'm growing to love them,' he admitted, thinking of the last time he'd seen Connie, music blaring, hugging Flea, talking at the top of her lungs on her precious cellphone. Smiling despite himself. 'They're a bit…spiky.'

'I was spiky, too.'

'I can't imagine that.'

'Believe it,' she said. 'Have you contacted them yet to let them know you're safe?'

'They didn't know I was unsafe,' he said. 'We've hardly been missing for weeks.'

But the thought gave him pause.

He needed to take more precautions, he conceded. In their own way, Connie and Richard still needed him. He had responsibilities.

He looked at Rachel and wondered if he was ready for more.

The chopper was coming in to land—the chopper that'd take them back to the cruise ship.

'So you've decided?' he said softly. 'You've decided that you trust me enough to spend the next few days with me—and with forty other passengers?' And then, with the air of a man offering expensive chocolates, he held out his lure. 'And with lots of rocks.'

'Rocks,' she said reverently, and she grinned. 'How can you doubt I'm coming back?'

And, with that, she went to hug her sister goodbye and restart her holiday.

CHAPTER TEN

IF ANYONE had told Maud that Rachel's experience would have done her good she'd have told
them they had rocks in their heads.

She greeted her young friend with trepidation,
expecting her to be deeply traumatised. She'd
talked with her by radio before she'd come back
to the ship.

'Are you sure you want to go on? We could
both be taken off and flown on to Broome.'

'No way.' Rachel's response was emphatic.
'I'm not letting those druggies spoil more of our
holiday.'

'You're not coming back just for me?'

'No,' Rachel said and there was a thoughtful
pause. 'I'm coming back for me.'

But, after seeing her, Maud was thinking there
was a fair amount of Finn Kinnard thrown into
that equation as well.

Nothing like tossing a girl overboard with a

guy with a smile to die for, she thought. Nothing like leaving her on a deserted island for two days to put the colour back in her cheeks.

It was a nonsensical thought, but colour was definitely back in Rachel's cheeks. Her whole body language had changed.

She greeted Maud with joy. She slept the clock round, even missing two shore excursions to let her body recover, and then she bounced back, determined to take every inch of enjoyment from this cruise.

Especially when Finn was around.

She needed to keep her heart under control.

That was what Rachel kept telling herself, but she could do no such thing. This man had held her naked while she'd let terror overtake her. This man had swum beside her when she'd thought she'd die.

This man made her smile.

Caution.

For there was a tiny voice in the back of her mind saying, *Ramón, Ramón, Ramón. You were a fool once. You married a man you didn't know. You married a man you shouldn't have trusted.*

But Ramón was Ramón. And Finn was…Finn.

She knew so little about him. She wished she'd met him in Darwin, at the university where she was about to start teaching. She could ask people about him. He could take her home to meet these kids he talked about. Only his kids were back in the US. His life was back in the US, and she knew nothing.

She needed a private investigator to check him out.

Did she distrust her judgement that much?

Yes, she did, she conceded. When Finn wasn't around she knew her instincts were flawed. But when he was…

When he was he made her happy, simple as that. When he was with her, it was as if the nightmares of the past took their rightful place— a part of what she was but not a part that was blocking her future. Not a part that was a leaden weight, stopping her from living.

'Are you up to a bit of cliff climbing today?' It was Jason, newly graduated to head tour guide in Esme's stead. He was a great kid, and he thought Rachel was cool. 'I'm taking a group from the river mouth to the inland falls. You can climb up and swim in the rock pools above if you want. And on the way...' he hesitated '...there are some magnificent rock formations. We'd love it if you could tell the group how they were made.'

'Of course she will.' And Finn was right beside her, back in his customary shorts and T-shirt, back with his customary grin. 'You should put this lady on the payroll. I love listening to her talking about rocks.'

'So...you're coming?' she asked him a trifle breathlessly, and his smile softened.

'"Whither thou goest, I will go,"' he quoted softly.

'Finn...'

'I know,' he said a trifle ruefully. 'It's far too soon. But it's not too soon to climb a waterfall and have a swim.'

He was here to watch the crew.

He'd watched them.

There were a couple more crew members whose obvious nervousness meant that questioning when they reached Broome was a no-brainer. For the rest, though, investigation was done. He was Finn Kinnard, a guy on holiday, a guy who'd met a woman who was everything he'd ever dreamed of.

Or not.

For he'd never dreamed of a woman like this. He hadn't known such a woman existed.

He climbed the falls with her. He listened to Jason ask about the rock formations and he watched as passengers clustered around to hear her answers.

She made these rocks come alive. The layer on layer of time-tortured sediment told a story, and Rachel gave it a voice.

The passengers loved her.

He loved her.

Jason pointed out the rock pools. Above the falls there were scores, connected by a web of waterways.

Fresh water, safe—and private.

Jason was taking most of the walkers to look at caves further inland, and he warned the younger ones that if they wanted to explore the pools they were on their own.

'We call this place Honeymoon Hotel,' he said and chuckled. 'There are scores of waterholes, all beautifully separated. It's a stiff climb but it's safe and it's worth it. Rule is, you claim a waterhole and you don't go near the others. I'll whistle when it's time to leave. I'll whistle ten minutes before I come and find you. No matter what you're doing, make sure you listen for that whistle. I'll be back in an hour.'

Amid general laughter, the main group disappeared, leaving...the honeymooners. And Rachel and Finn who just happened to decide—independently—without even looking at each other—that it sounded okay by them.

She should go on with Maud, Rachel thought, but she glanced at Maud and Maud grinned and waved goodbye and the thing was decided. Finn took her hand and she let him lead—wherever he wanted to take her.

They climbed and what they found at the top was worth the struggle. It was worth letting Finn help her up the steep scree. Acknowledging she needed help and acknowledging she didn't mind leaning on this man.

It was even worth the reaction from the rest of the passengers that they were now an acknowledged couple.

* * *

Finn had been here before. He knew the best pool—the one furthest from anywhere, at the far reaches of Jason's whistle. He led Rachel to its edge, and she stared in fascination into its depths.

The low sun-burned bush-scape gave each pool privacy and she could hear giggles and whoops from afar as each couple figured that here was unexpected freedom on such a supervised tour. For there was nothing except crystal-clear water—and bush-land for privacy—and rocks.

Rachel looked into the pool's depths as if she was looking at rock structure. She *was* looking at rock structure.

'I can feel a lecture coming on,' Finn groaned, and grinned and tugged off his T-shirt and slid down into the depths. He sank until his feet hit the sandy bottom, then surfaced right by where Rachel was sitting. He hauled himself part way out of the water, looked attentively up at her and cocked his head. 'Go ahead, miss, I'm all ears. What are we looking at?'

'Rocks.'

'What else?'

'And water.'

'I've come all this way to learn that?'

'You need to start somewhere.'

'Ah, but you've already taught me stuff. I thought I'd graduated to Rocks 102.'

'Not if you're going to mock me.'

'I would never mock you.'

'You'd laugh at me.'

'I'd laugh with you,' he said softly. 'There is a difference.'

She looked down at him for a long, long moment. Things were changing between them. He was asking her to trust, he thought, and for this woman it was a big ask.

What was going on in her head? How much had that creep of a husband hurt her?

To lose a child... He couldn't begin to fathom such loss. Such hurt.

He'd never hurt as she had. He'd never known such grief.

His mother had been bruised by one ghastly betrayal and never got over it. She'd been a shadow on the periphery of his life, and her death had been a loss but not a gut-wrenching grief.

His grandparents were different—there was never a doubt that they loved him and he loved them right back—but they were middle-aged when they'd had their only daughter, and by the time Finn was born they were already approaching old age.

Their deaths had been a natural attrition, timely, and although he'd grieved for them, he hadn't felt aching loss.

A loss such as Rachel had faced.

He looked up at Rachel now and he thought he didn't know how to deal with it. He didn't know how she could deal with it.

If she'd been his mother or his grandmother, she'd have wilted without trace.

But Rachel wasn't wilting.

For suddenly Rachel's expression changed. Some inner decision had been reached. Before he realised what she intended, she slipped, fully clothed, into the water beside him.

She looped her arms around his neck and she tilted her chin.

'I know there's a difference,' she said softly.

'It's just sometimes I can't remember. I need to be reminded.'

'How can I remind you?'

'If you can't guess,' she said softly, 'then 102 is way beyond your intelligence. Try.'

So what was a man to do but stop thinking—and try?

How could a man not?

To convince her he was serious… To convince her she was special… There was only one action that could possibly meet the criteria.

A kiss.

So do it.

What followed was some very serious silence while they explored this kiss. It was different to the kisses they'd exchanged on the island. Those had been kisses of isolation, of fear, of need.

This was a kiss of exploration, an acknowledgement that this could be the beginning of a future that was not all about terror and mutual comfort.

It was far, far more than that.

For this woman did something to him that he'd never experienced. She hadn't bothered with a swimsuit—why, when clothes dried on you in half an hour? She was wearing shorts and her customary oversized shirt, but in the water they seemed almost to disappear.

He'd caught her as she'd slipped into the water. He held her around her waist and he could feel her body against his. He could feel every lovely curve of her, and she felt…she felt as if she was melting into him.

She felt as if she was part of him.

Her mouth was on his and it was Rachel who was doing the kissing, Rachel who was doing the demanding. She was pressuring his mouth to open, demanding to explore, and he let her do what she willed, glorying in her assertiveness, glorying in this woman he'd so wrongly stereotyped.

She wanted him—and he wanted her right back.

If the water had been deep they could have drowned, he thought, for surely he didn't have attention left to pay to such detail as breathing. As it was, he was shoulder-deep in water, deep enough to support her, to hold her to him, to fold her into him and kiss her and kiss her and kiss her.

He heard her whimper, and it was as if it came from a long way away. Her hands were in his hair, dragging him to her, deepening the kiss, desperate to be close.

Deeper and deeper... Closer and closer...

He was turning slowly in the water, and her legs were around his hips. Her whole body clung. Her whole body was surrendering.

'Finn...' It was a desperate, ragged whisper between kisses, and he felt his whole body shudder in recognition of naked need.

'I can't...we should have... Oh, Finn, I want you.' Her words were half spoken, half understood, for her claim to him was growing more fierce by the moment. 'I want...'

And so did he. His hands were under her shirt, inside the cups of her bra, feeling the fullness, the taut, aching need...

He'd never wanted anything more than he wanted Rachel at this moment.

He'd never want anything again.

The water was cool, which was just as well, as his body was burning and his brain had misted into an opaque fog where the only thing he knew was his desire.

Rachel…

'We can't…Finn, we can't…' It was a sigh of despair—and it was enough for the mist to clear. For just a moment. Just.

'I believe,' he managed, in a voice ragged with want, 'that my wallet's lying up there on the rock.'

'Your wallet…' Somehow she managed to pull away, just a little. She was still holding close and her legs weren't loosening their hold. Her nose was two inches from his. 'Is there…maybe a corner store around here where we can buy what we need?'

'I might have packed what we need,' he admitted, wondering how she'd take it. 'I mean… they're the sort of things most single guys carry with them—in case.'

'You didn't have them on the island.' She sounded stunned.

'I forgot to ask if I could go back to my cabin and fetch my wallet before they threw us overboard,' he told her. 'Stupid, I know. Does today make up for it?'

'As in…making up for it by telling me you have condoms in your wallet.'

'Condom,' he said mournfully. 'I wasn't *that* hopeful.'

'So…just once?' she whispered, awed.

'Before Jason blows his whistle.'

'He said maybe an hour.' Her legs were tightening even further and her hands… Her hands…

He was losing his mind here.

'An hour,' he said and groaned and fell backward into the water so she was floating on top of him. Each of them was doing what they must— and only what they must—to stay afloat but it was a joint effort.

They'd fused and he wasn't letting go.

'I need to reach my wallet,' he murmured and she sighed and kissed him until they did go under and had to surface to splutter and find air.

'My wallet—and air,' he managed.

'Air's optional,' she managed back. 'But the wallet… Tell you what… You see that nice sandy bank ten feet away?'

'Barely.'

'Try,' she said. 'Try very hard. It's important.'

'Because?'

'Because it's a rendezvous point,' she told him. 'The best Boy Scouts always plan ahead and I know I'm not a Boy Scout but I'm planning anyway. If we get separated, we make our way individually to the rendezvous point.'

'Sounds a plan,' he said, and kissed her for good measure. 'Should we agree on a time?'

'How about as soon as possible?' she murmured. 'How about as soon as you find what's in that wallet and as soon as I can figure how to get this bra undone?'

'No need,' he said and kissed her long and deep, with an aching, sensual pleasure he'd never felt before and had no idea he was capable of feeling. 'Even Cub Scouts are taught fastenings. I am so prepared.'

'Not until you have that wallet,' she murmured and pushed him away. 'Now. Fast.'

'Yes, ma'am,' he said and swam hard to the rock where he'd left his wallet, found what he needed and turned back to her.

To find—she'd done all her unfastening herself.

The sight took his breath away—the woman he desired more than anything in the world, naked on the sand, half in and half out of the water.

'We're on whistle deadline,' she said and she

smiled across the waterhole at him, making his heart twist. Making all of him twist. 'Come to me,' she said.

And he did.

The whistle was delayed. Whether the caves proved more interesting than expected, or whether Jason was a true romantic, who could say? All Rachel knew was that Finn's one condom was stretched to the limit and she'd never felt so happy. Ever.

They were lying on the soft sun-warmed sand, half in and half out of the water, sated with loving. 'We look like crumbed rissoles,' Finn said lovingly, who knew when, and they rolled back into the water and washed off their coating and then proceeded to put it back on.

She felt warm, sleepy, sated—wonderful. She felt loved. She lay in Finn's arms, she felt his heartbeat under hers and she felt as if she'd never known until now what happiness was.

He was true, she thought blissfully. Her one true thing.

With Ramón, even as she'd married him, she'd

known he'd kept a part of himself apart. 'I'm an artist,' he'd told her. 'I need personal space.'

That personal space, she'd found out later, hadn't been filled with solitude.

He'd smashed her trust. He'd killed her baby, and she'd thought she could never trust again.

She could never love again.

And here she was…loving.

She stirred in Finn's arms and he tugged her closer and kissed her so deeply she felt she should melt. She'd never felt this close to a man. She'd never felt this close…

'Maybe Jason's whistle's broken,' she whispered and she felt his chuckle rather than heard it.

'What a tragedy. Let's not care. We have fresh water, I can build fires and you can cook lizards. What more do we want?'

'We might run out of sunscreen after a while,' she managed, and wriggled closer still. Skin against skin… It was the most erotic sensation in the world. 'And there is the matter of just one condom.'

'I was prepared,' he said, sounding wounded.

'Just not prepared enough. Who could expect I'd meet a nymph like you in a place like this?'

'Seeing you brought your nymph with you...'

'There is that,' he said and kissed her again. 'But I'm even more prepared than last time. I also have a satellite phone on my belt. I can ring for an air drop.'

'Of condoms?'

'That's the one.'

She giggled. 'Can you imagine the cost of getting one carton airlifted to the northern tip of the Kimberley? And what do we pay with? Barbecued lizards?'

'I have my credit card.' He'd ceased kissing her lips. He was kissing other places. Lower. Lower.

She was on fire, her whole body screaming its need to be closer...closer...

'I suspect...I suspect even with credit cards it might be out of the range of one hasn't-been-employed-for-a-year geologist and one security officer,' she whispered. 'Oh, Finn...'

But he paused. His kisses ceased and he shifted so he held her loosely, his arms around her waist. They were curved together on the soft sand. Far above, an osprey wheeled lazily in the thermals, but beyond there was nothing.

There were more rock pools, more couples but in this magic place sound didn't travel. Nothing travelled.

He couldn't do this, he thought. Even though the condom had been in his wallet, he hadn't thought it would go this far.

He'd never dreamed she could love him so completely.

She had. She did. She'd told him everything about herself, and he...he hadn't been honest.

If he was to love this woman—and he did—the time to be honest was right now.

Now and for ever...

'We might be the first man and the first woman...' Rachel whispered and then she saw Finn's expression. 'What's wrong?'

'Rachel, love, I need to tell you something,' he said. 'What you said just then... Enough. I should have been honest with you earlier. I didn't intend...that we get this close so soon.'

'You're about to tell me you're married?' She'd

meant it to be a joke, but it came out a bit breath-less, a bit scared. His expression said something was wrong. 'Finn?'

'I'm not married, Rachel,' he told her. 'But I have been less than honest. I'm not a security officer.'

There was a silence. A silence that stretched and stretched. She looked at him for a long time, studying his face. Trying to work things out.

'Then you're a cop,' she said at last. 'You said...'

'I said I wasn't a cop.'

'Then what?' Why did it matter? He could be an idle dilettante, she thought and it shouldn't matter.

It shouldn't.

'I own the cruise line,' he said and her world stilled.

'You own...'

'I own the *Kimberley Temptress*, plus eight other cruise ships. My father inherited ships from my grandfather. Big ships. He pretty much gambled and womanised away his fortune, but there was enough left at the end for me to con-solidate into this line.'

She let his words sink in. The stillness was suddenly oppressive, loaded with menace. It was as if her past had suddenly crashed into this perfect morning, and it was all around her.

She watched his face, and she thought this shouldn't matter. But then, overriding sense, memories slammed back, as unwanted as they were uncalled for.

'So I lied? What's the big deal? This is the truth, now, Rachel, baby. You can believe this.'

Ramón, lying and lying, over and over again. *You can believe this.*

'You…you lied?' It was as much as she could do to get the words out, but, as she managed it, the pain of the last few years slammed back with a force that felt like a physical blow. She'd thought never to say those words again. She'd sworn never to be in the position to need to.

'I didn't lie…'

'That's semantics,' she snapped because she knew this ruse, too. *I didn't lie…* Sometimes Ramón hadn't. Sometimes he'd led her to assume things.

'You made me believe you were a security officer,' she whispered.

'I inherited my father's fortune,' he said. 'It changed my life. I came on this cruise undercover to try and figure what was happening on the ship, so in a sense I have been a security officer. But there's more. There's a deeper reason I haven't been honest. Rachel, for some dumb reason…as soon as I got to know you, I wanted to be like I was before. Finn Kinnard, boat-builder, making my own way. I know I can't go back to that. I know it shouldn't matter, but it seemed… what was between us was too important to mess with by telling you what I owned.'

'You told me what you thought I wanted to hear?'

'No.'

'You did,' she said, suddenly bleak. 'I'm used to that.'

'Rachel…'

'You're right, it shouldn't matter,' she whispered. 'It shouldn't change anything, that you let me believe you're a security officer. How is it that everything in me is screaming that it does?'

And, before he could respond, she rolled back into the water, diving under its clear depths and swimming strongly across to the ledge where her clothes lay. She needed distance. She needed to get away from the nightmare of those memories.

They were overwhelming. They made her feel ill.

The nightmares were nothing to do with Finn—but she couldn't escape them.

She hauled herself out of the water and tugged on shorts and shirt with hands that wouldn't stop trembling.

'Rachel…' He swam across to join her but he didn't emerge from the water. He held the rock at her feet and looked up at her. 'Rachel, it's no big deal.'

Of all the things he could have said, it needed only that.

No big deal. One deception.

Two deceptions.

He'd lied about his kids. She knew the reason for that.

She knew the reason but she didn't have to like it. And this?

He was explaining again why he'd lied. It even made sense. Sort of. To her head, but not to her heart. If she stayed here he'd explain it all, she thought numbly. He'd explain it reasonably, calmly, making her feel foolish for worrying about being lied to.

Just as Ramón had.

But she was tired of feeling foolish. More, she was sick to death of deception.

She stared down at him and thought, I've just made love to a guy I thought I knew.

He owned this cruise line?

She knew the line. The ships were fabulous. If Maud hadn't brought her she'd never have been able to afford to be a passenger.

He owned it?

How many cruises had he taken?

How many stupid women had he picked up along the way?

She was being unfair. This was Finn. *Finn.* She knew him. Her heart knew him. He wouldn't…

How did she know he wouldn't?

She'd lost her baby by not knowing. By letting her heart rule her head.

By wanting to believe.

And then she heard a whistle. Signalling the end?

She closed her eyes, wanting to block out pain,

shock, betrayal. Not just the pain and betrayal of now, but the pain and betrayal of life.

'Rachel, don't look like that.' He swung himself out of the water and went to hold her but she backed away.

'I don't want…' she managed, her breath coming in painful gasps. 'I don't want anything to do with liars.'

'You know there are reasons.' He sounded logical, she thought. Maybe he thought she was being hysterical.

Maybe she was, but she couldn't help it. She was suddenly back in a bleak hospital room, looking down at her tiny daughter, seeing where deception ended.

'Leave me be,' she said, her voice dead and empty. 'When Ramón killed our baby and did his best to destroy me I made a vow—that nothing or no one would ever get that close again. For a while, here, now, I forgot that vow but that doesn't mean it ceases. I've slipped up and now I'm back in control.'

She paused and looked away, down into the depths of the rock pool, as if searching for answers.

'I've had a lovely morning,' she said, her voice becoming gentle. 'That's...that's how I want to remember it. A magic morning in a magic place. I fell in love with your body, but the rest of you...I know you can explain your deception. I know it shouldn't matter, but it does. It does in such a huge way I can't begin to describe it. Logical or not, I need to walk away. Maud will say I'm crazy. Maybe *I* will say I'm crazy, but I don't want rich, and I don't want deception. So I guess...I guess, Finn Kinnard, that means I don't want you.'

CHAPTER ELEVEN

NOTHING would sway her. Nothing he could say. Nothing anyone could say. She retired into Rachel-the-Geologist and she stayed there for the rest of the journey.

To his astonishment and frustration—and envy—she even managed to enjoy herself, but she enjoyed herself without him.

She withdrew from him. She made no drama of it. She was civil, even pleasant, but when he greeted her she responded with no warmth, simply a reserve he couldn't reach.

In desperation he even turned to Maud. Told her all. Waited for her verdict.

When it came, it was bleak.

'I can see why you lied. She's talked to me about it, and I can understand the reasons and I can tell her I understand. They even make sense,' she said bluntly. 'But this is Rachel we're talking about, a woman who's been lied to until her life was almost destroyed. She's not any woman, Mr Kinnard, she's Rachel, and although underneath she's one tough woman, she's been given a life lesson she'll never forget. And yes, I know your lies weren't bald whoppers, but you set out to deceive her. What you haven't figured is that she doesn't need you. She's just learning to be herself again. She has no reason to take you on trust—why should she? I suggest you get on with running your cruise line and forget her.'

'I've fallen in love with her,' he said, because with Maud nothing less than the absolute truth would do. If it could do anything.

Maud's expression said maybe it couldn't.

'Why wouldn't you?' she said, her stern face becoming gentle. 'She's one amazing woman. But if you've fallen in love with her then you have an uphill battle to prove yourself and I can't tell you where to start.'

'I've blown it,' he said bleakly and she nodded.

'Yes,' she said. 'I believe you have.'

Montgomery Reef was one of the most awesome places in the world, and nothing was going to mess with the ship's timetable here. The last cruise had missed the reef emerging from the sea because of Esme and her appalling alternative agenda, but this time the ship was anchored early, a hundred yards from the reef, waiting for low tide. Waiting for the miracle.

Not that you'd know it. From where the ship was anchored, the sea was a vast calm expanse with nothing marring its flatness.

The reef was four yards underwater at high tide, and two yards above at low tide. At high tide there was nothing to see. But, as the tide fell, the ten mile mass of reef emerged, like the Loch Ness Monster, vast and mysterious and a thousand times more amazing than any prehistoric fantasy.

Finn had seen it before but it never ceased to awe him, the vast reef emerging from the sea, the great solid reef becoming a huge plateau, with every side a massive waterfall as the reef's surface oozed its water back into the ocean.

It was breathtaking, but what he was watching this time was Rachel's reaction.

She'd been quiet since their time at the rock pool, but she was still determined to take every ounce of enjoyment from this cruise. She and

Maud stood together at the ship's rail and watched the reef slowly rise to the surface, break the clear water and then rise still further.

Turtles were everywhere. They must be feeding on the tiny fishes slipping from the reef's surface. Standing on the lower deck of the *Temptress,* you could almost lean over and touch them as they flippered past.

Rachel was truly awed. He watched her face and thought he wanted to be standing beside her, feeling her amazement. She said something to Maud and made her smile. How could he be jealous of an eighty-three-year-old woman?

He was jealous.

She wanted nothing more to do with him.

He had to leave her alone.

He'd figured a strategy—of a sort. Pressure now would get him nowhere. He needed to wait, take the pressure off, then maybe in a few weeks, when she was settled in her job in Darwin, he'd contact her, do a bit of apologetic grovelling and say, *Can we start again?*

It was the only strategy he could think of.

It seemed a lousy strategy.

Jason was helping Maud and Rachel into an inflatable dinghy—after an hour being briefed on how not to hurt the reef's delicate eco-structure, passengers were being ferried onto its surface.

'One seat left,' Jason called. 'You, Finn…'

'Right.' He stepped into the dinghy and the only seat was beside Rachel.

'You two seem to have had a tiff,' Jason said, and grinned as he gunned the little boat away from the *Temptress* towards the reef. Away from Esme's dour influence the young tour guide was a lot more confident—and he was growing cheeky. 'No tiffs on my ship. Kiss and make up.'

'Kissing transmits germs,' Rachel said equitably, as if it didn't matter at all that she'd just been told to kiss. 'I'll shake hands instead. Good afternoon, Mr Kinnard. Do sit down and look at turtles.'

He sat amid laughter from the rest of the passengers. He looked at turtles, and at the stunning emergence of the reef. They cruised the length of the reef and it was like cruising the face of a vast elongated waterfall.

Maud was in the seat in front, talking avidly to Jason.

Rachel was intent on turtles.

He had to lean across her to see. Inadvertently, he touched her.

He felt her flinch and he thought she was acting impervious but there was no way she was feeling as tough as she looked.

He'd hurt her. Badly.

Another woman might react well, he thought wryly, to the news that the guy who loved her was wealthy. But this was Rachel, who'd learned the hard way not to trust her heart.

'I'm sorry,' he murmured and she kept right on turtle-watching.

'I'm sorry, too,' she said. 'It shouldn't be such a big deal but it is. Have you been on this reef before?'

'I...yes.'

'Nothing special, then.'

'I think you could call this trip special,' he said dryly.

'You mean you don't get tossed overboard every time?'

'Or get to meet you.'

'We're not going down that road,' she said sternly, and he had a sudden vision of her in her new life as a university lecturer. The vision made him blink. It was…sexy, he conceded.

But then, everything about Rachel was sexy.

'Did you know all that stuff I spouted about rocks?' she asked suddenly. 'Do you know that, too? Were you just interested to humour me?'

'Yep,' he said. 'I know it all.'

She swung round from her turtles and faced him, astonished. Then, as he raised one brow, mock questioning, her lips twitched.

'That's another lie.'

'I'm incorrigible.'

'Finn…'

'I know,' he said. 'I *am* incorrigible. But I'm also repentant. Maybe in time…'

'Maybe,' she said but she went back to her turtles and he thought her maybe was a lie all on its own.

The reef stunned her. They were permitted two hours' exploration before the tide changed and the reef sank again into the depths.

Jason and the new tour guide, an eager lass called Marie, watched them every minute, but the passengers had been well briefed. Take nothing but photographs and don't even leave footprints. Watch as you put each foot down to make sure there's not some delicate form of reef-life underfoot. They knew the rules. Within half an hour Jason had relaxed enough to allow the passengers to do their own thing, and Rachel could wander from the group and explore alone.

Which was a luxury on a cruise like this. Solitude.

The reef was alive with life, but she needed to look to find it. From the ship, Montgomery Reef looked a great gleaming slab of grey rock. But up close… They called it the upside down reef, for that was what it was. Everything was hidden from the fierce tropical sun, but underneath was a mass of hiding places.

She turned a rock and the colours took her breath away. The giant clams lurking in the depths of the rock pools were harvesting their food—during this time out of water tiny sea creatures were trapped and the clams found their feed. There were fishes and crabs and corals, and so many different types of rock formation she felt as if she could sit down and write a thesis.

If she could stop thinking about Finn Kinnard.

He was talking to Maud. Maud was asking him something—pointing to something in a rock pool.

Maud was the only passenger who knew who he was. He could relax with her.

He could relax with me, she thought, and tried to put the thought away.

It stayed.

Why couldn't she just go with it? Why couldn't she walk—carefully—back to them and see what it was they were talking about? Smile at Finn, like Maud was smiling at him?

Why couldn't she let him into her heart?

Because she didn't trust her heart, and she wasn't going there again.

'Dumb or not,' she said out loud, and she was far enough away from the group to decide a little conversation with herself was permissible. It was something she'd missed during the cruise—the daily chats to tell herself how she was going, what the next step should be, how to keep putting one foot after another.

Without those chats, her feet had just…stepped, right into Finn Kinnard's arms.

'That's what happens when you let your guard down,' she told herself. 'You walk right into a drug bust, you get thrown overboard, you end up castaway and you imagine you're in love.'

'I'm not in love,' she told herself harshly. 'I'm not.'

She glanced again at Maud—and at Finn. He looked… He looked…

'Dangerous,' she said out loud, and she stared down into the rock pool and saw a tiny orange and black fish swim too close to the clam's giant jaws.

She saw the jaws slide shut.

She shuddered.

'You thought that clam was a rock,' she whispered to the now-gone fish. 'You trusted. That was dumb.'

It was dumb.

She was being stupid. She was in one of the most beautiful places in the world and the most inaccessible—and she was wasting time behaving like a lovesick teenager.

'Put him out of your mind, take some photographs and enjoy yourself,' she told herself harshly. 'Now.'

She tried.
A girl had to be sensible.
A girl had no choice.

CHAPTER TWELVE

THE ship docked at Broome on a hot, still Monday morning. Passengers were disembarking, heading to yet more adventures or to the airport to fly home.

Finn watched as each passenger was presented with a magnificent hamper, along with postage vouchers if they wished to send the hamper home, as apology for the drama during the cruise.

With its happy ending, the drama would do nothing but good, he thought. It would achieve national press coverage. Maybe international. Past passengers would read about it and previous problems would be explained. The *Kimberley Temptress*'s future was assured.

That press coverage could be problematic, though. His cover was now well and truly blown. As soon as passengers disembarked they'd learn that Finn Kinnard was Fineas J Sunderson, owner of the Temptress Line.

It didn't matter. Rachel already knew.

And he could head to the airport and go home.

But Rachel and Maud were staying in Broome for another week. Maud had told him that.

Maud was on his side. She knew he'd messed up but she was hoping he might be able to fix it.

One week…or wait for months and then come back and visit Rachel in Darwin?

One week…

'So this is goodbye.' Rachel was smiling at him, determinedly cheerful, holding out her hand in farewell.

'No,' he said and her smile died.

'Finn…'

'I need to spend time with the police,' he said. 'They'll want a statement from you as well. Maybe together…'

'There's no need for together.'

'Where are you staying?' Maud was nattily dressed, ready for offshore adventures, beaming at the two of them. Despite the dramas, the cruise seemed to have done her good.

He told her and her beam widened. 'Isn't this a coincidence? We'll see you by the pool, then—or on a camel. I've heard there are awesome camel rides along the beach at sunset.'

'Mr Kinnard will be too busy to sit by the pool or ride camels,' Rachel said repressively. 'He's here on business.'

But greater forces were at work here. Finn had cleverly discovered where they were staying— simply by asking Maud. Maud now looked innocence personified, and he thought there were lies and lies. He knew he might very well see Rachel again by the pool—or on a camel. By accident or by design.

'I would like to see you again,' he said gently to Rachel, and she flushed.

'There's no point.'

'Isn't there?' He met her gaze full on, almost a challenge, and watched while her flush deepened.

'Don't,' she muttered.

'I won't. If that's what you really want...'

'It's what I have to want,' she said savagely. 'I'm not being stupid for a second time.'

'Rachel, he's all over the Internet. The press is going crazy. It seems he's been really reclusive but this brought him out into the open—and he sounds lovely.'

'Finn?' Of course it was Finn. They were settling into their luxury resort at Broome. Rachel had unpacked and washed her hair, then come through their adjoining suite door to find Maud on her laptop. Someone should tell Maud that eighty-three was too old to dive into computing, she thought bitterly, but Maud had taken to it like a duck to water and had suffered two weeks' Internet withdrawal. She was now reading international newspapers online. About Finn.

'His real name is Fineas Sunderson,' she said.

'He's not even using his real name?' She said it with bitterness.

'Well, he is, sort of,' Maud conceded and, despite herself, Rachel sat on the bed and looked at the screen. 'It says here his father didn't have any legitimate children. When he died he left the whole shipping line to Finn, on condition that he change his name.'

'Lucky Finn.'

'It says there are three known illegitimate children,' Maud said, reading on. 'This is from a newspaper article in Maine—the journalist has done some real probing. The castaway story has caught the public imagination and she's delved for background. According to the article, the old man left the line to Finn either because he was a boat-builder or because he was the oldest but Finn had no greater claim than the other two. So Finn's taken over the line but he's splitting the profits three ways.'

Rachel stilled at that. She was remembering Finn's hands. She thought of him as a boat-building apprentice, starting young... She thought of him taking on a cruise line and supporting siblings...

'You can't believe all you read,' she managed and Maud gave her a thoughtful look.

'You can't disbelieve it, either.'

'Maud...'

'Do you really want to let him go?'

'He lied.'

'He was doing a job, Rachel,' Maud said gently.

'He wasn't doing a job when he was on the island.'

'How would you have reacted?' Maud demanded. 'If he'd told you he was rich, that he owned the ship and that his crew had put you in that position?'

She tried to consider. She tried to be honest. 'I might have reacted badly,' she admitted.

'Finn's done two things for us,' Maud said with asperity. 'First, he saved me from a watery grave.'

'Anyone would have done that,' she retorted. 'He just got in first—and, besides, he pushed you in.'

'He didn't push me in. He bumped me in when I tripped—and there's something very comforting about a man who gets in first.' Maud was speaking out in Finn's defence and, as a defence lawyer, she made a good one. 'And then there's you. He didn't have to leap out of the shadows and put himself in harm's way, ending up on that island.'

'It was *his* crew...'

'He didn't have to put himself in harm's way,' Maud repeated. 'Did he?'

'N... No.'

'He wasn't drug-running himself.'

'No, but all that time at the island... *He's rich*!'

'And that's bad?'

'He didn't tell me,' she said flatly. 'He let me believe he was an employee. I won't be lied to.'

Maud looked thoughtful. She glanced down at the navy and white polka dotted swimsuit she was wearing, and then she turned to the mirror. And winced. 'What do I look like in this?' she demanded.

'I…' Rachel stared at her, confused. 'Why?'

'Never mind why. Tell me!' She waited—including toe-tapping—for a response.

'Cute,' Rachel said at last—and then she coloured.

'Precisely,' Maud said, glaring at her reflection and then at Rachel. 'The swimming costume might be cute but that's not what I asked. I'm an eighty-three-year-old in a swimming costume. Cute? Not so much. So was that a lie? You decide. Rachel, don't you let one moronic husband make you stick to black and white all your life. Sometimes grey is kind, necessary and even sensible. Think about it. For now, I've said all I have to say on the matter. I'm about to dip my body in the pool. Coming?'

'I…yes.'

'And if Finn's there, you will be civil to him?'

'Of course.'

'Kind?'

'Don't push it.'

'I won't push it,' Maud said grimly, but then she managed a smile. 'He *is* a boat-builder,' she said. 'He does know how to wield a hammer. Just think of him, out in the sun, building his wooden boat, stripped to the waist, sun glinting on his naked bronzed back…'

'Maud!'

'I'm just saying,' Maud said serenely. 'I'm just thinking bronze is an even better option than grey. I'm just saying you need to do some serious thinking. Now, pool, swim—come.'

He wasn't at the pool.

Finn spent almost all his first day in Broome closeted with the police. They needed to interview Rachel as well, but he persuaded them to let her be for a little. His evidence was damning enough to make hers less important—to give her space.

Would space help?

There was another problem. He'd hit the headlines—he and Rachel, both. If she hadn't known about him before she reached Darwin, she'd know now.

'*Shipping magnate and girlfriend thrown overboard—left for dead.*'

There was more—in-depth probing that made him cringe, and the press was hounding for more. Like who was his girlfriend?

At least the resort they were staying in was exclusive and knew how to protect its guests. Rachel could stay out of the limelight as long as she didn't appear in public—and as long as she didn't appear with him.

He phoned Connie and Richard, wanting them to find out before they saw it on TV. To his vague disquiet, they weren't answering—not even their cellphones.

He shouldn't worry. They had their own lives, he reminded himself. They were no longer the struggling kids he'd found when his father died. They'd always demanded their independence and he gave it to them, regardless of the occasional disquiet it caused.

If they were both away, his housekeeper might well have decided to visit her mother. He could ring her and check.

Why? Contrary to what he'd implied to Rachel—lied to Rachel?—they were adults. He expected them not to worry about him. Why worry about them?

Of course he worried. He cared about them more than he'd ever admit, but he'd embarrass them to death if he told them. They'd retreat right back into the shells they were wonderfully starting to emerge from.

Maybe he should go home.

He did need to spend time with the police here. He did need to spend time with his crew. But then… What was holding him?

Rachel was holding him. Rachel was on this side of the world.

Rachel was indifferent.

No. Not indifferent. Wounded.

In the next couple of days he gave information to the police, to customs and to the marine authorities. He got to know his new crew and made sure the *Temptress* would give the next lot of paying customers a cruise memorable for all the right reasons.

He thought about Rachel.

Rachel avoided him. Maud was sympathetic but there was nothing she could do. 'She knows she's being overly judgemental,' she said, meeting him at the breakfast bar. Rachel had disappeared the moment she saw him. 'But she's stuck. If Ramón had wounded just her, maybe she'd take a risk again, but it was her baby...'

'She wouldn't be taking a risk,' he growled and, before he knew it, he was being hugged. Which, with Maud, was quite some hug.

'No,' she said, releasing him and looking just a wee bit embarrassed. Conceding she'd overstepped the mark even for Maud. 'I know that, but I've lived in the world a lot longer than Rachel. She has to figure it out for herself.'

'She won't do that in a week.'

'No,' Maud said sorrowfully. 'I don't think she will.'

In which case, he might as well go back to the States, he thought morosely. He was making himself miserable here.

That evening he sat and watched the camels doing their nightly perambulation along the magnificent Cairns Beach, noticing that every camel held two. Couples. Mums and dads. Siblings. Friends. Finally, he saw Maud and Rachel swaying along on their beast.

They saw him and Maud waved fiercely and Rachel gave him a polite nod.

She'd be happier if he left, he thought.

Tonight he was taking the new captain of the *Kimberley Temptress* to supper. After that, he had one more thing to do.

Dinosaur footprints.

They were only to be seen when the tide was really low, and tomorrow morning the tide would be perfect. He'd never seen them—the twice he'd been to Broome before had coincided with higher tides—but now, for some reason, he found himself thinking of them.

He was thinking of a conversation with Rachel about what was important.

He could look at them at dawn, he decided. They'd remind him that in the fullness of time, relationships were nothing.

Then he could go home.

He was now a man with a plan. It wasn't a very good one, but he'd stick to it.

He had supper with the new captain at a hotel in town and, as he walked back through the foyer of the resort, he met Rachel and Maud, leaving the resort restaurant.

Maud beamed a welcome. Rachel gave him a strained smile.

His plan said it was time to say goodbye.

'I wanted to find you,' he told them. He'd intended to let them know tomorrow but it might as well be now. 'I'm returning to the States. I'll need to return for the court case but my plane's at midday tomorrow.' He hesitated, thinking of all the things he wanted to say; thinking of the few things he could.

Watching Rachel's face. Wishing…

No. Move on. Stick to the plan.

'What was done to you…' he began. 'The stress you both went through…I can't begin to tell you how sorry I am.' And then he met Rachel's gaze directly. 'And I can't begin to tell you how sorry I am that I've hurt you.'

'You haven't hurt her,' Maud muttered. 'She's being silly.'

'She has every right…'

'To be silly?' Rachel managed. 'Thanks very much.' She glowered at Maud but she managed to turn it into a smile to him. Polite but distant.

'You haven't ridden your camel yet—or seen your dinosaur footprints.'

'I've seen you riding your camel,' he said. 'That'll have to do. Maybe I'll see you in Darwin. Maybe…'

'Maybe…' Her words trailed off as well.

There was nothing left to say, Finn thought. Leave.

But then…

'Finn!'

The shout came from across the foyer, making Rachel start. A girl was launching herself across the foyer like a whirlwind. She was a swirl of rainbow, dressed in masses of multicoloured fabric. Her blonde curls were flying everywhere. Her eyes were lined heavily with black. Her lips were bright red and a tattoo of tiny bees ran up both arms. She looked young and funky and… breathtaking.

She twined herself around Finn so he was almost enveloped, hugging and kissing and weeping, all at the same time.

'Hey, don't smother him.'

A guy was strolling more sedately up to join

them. He was blond as well, but taller, dressed all in black, in heavy boots, skinny jeans and T-shirt, and with a skull earring in one ear. He looked almost too young to be sporting the not-very-thick beard attached to his face, but his smile was familiar. Very familiar. 'Connie, let go and give us guys a chance,' he said.

The girl gasped and sniffed and pulled back, then searched desperately for something to wipe her eyes and nose.

Maud obliged, with one of her endless supply of handkerchiefs emblazoned with the Thurston monogram. The girl looked down at it in aston-ishment, then grinned and blew her nose.

Meanwhile, the guy was man-hugging Finn, looking almost as emotional as the girl.

'We had to come,' he said as he finally pulled away. 'Man, Finn, you've given us a fright. When we read the papers and figured where you'd been stuck... And then we read that in-depth thing the journalist wrote...Connie was beside herself.'

And suddenly the atmosphere changed. It intensified, from relief to accusation. Connie lowered the Thurston handkerchief and tried to glare, while Rachel and Maud looked on, too stunned to move.

'Is it true our father didn't leave us anything?' she demanded, and Rachel thought, *We shouldn't be here.*

'Maud...' she started, backing away.

But... 'Guys, this is Rachel,' Finn said, grasping her hand and drawing her close, almost as if he were using her as a shield. 'And this is Dame Maud Thurston. Rachel, Maud, these are my half-sister and brother, Connie and Richard. Guys, Rachel is the woman who came overboard with me.'

'You're not kids,' Rachel managed.

'Hi, Rachel,' Connie said. 'Hi, Dame Maud.' But her greeting was perfunctory. 'And no, we're not kids, though Finn keeps acting as if we are. Just because we were feeble when he met us... Just because we needed him so badly...'

And then she seemed to collect herself. Maud's handkerchief had done its job. She was moving onto whatever it was that was bothering her.

'Finn, that journalist... She did a really intensive search of your background—it's in all the tabloids. We know you keep a low profile, but you're exposed now. Millionaire shipping magnate... Chief of the Temptress Line. That's fine; we knew that. But what we didn't know was the terms of our father's will. You told us...'

'That Dad's money was to be put into a family trust,' Richard said just as accusingly. 'That you're the trustee, but it's shared between us.'

'But now this journalist says it's not true,' Connie said, growing louder. 'The paper says it was all left to you. She got a copy of the will. She's talking about the *magnanimous* Fineas Sunderson.'

'I'm Finn Kinnard,' Finn said mildly. 'You know that. But magnanimous? You know me better than that.' He tried a grin. 'I'm lousy as anything.'

'So why did you lie about the will?' Connie demanded, refusing to be deflected.

Finn's smile faded. He looked as if he was backed against a wall, Rachel thought. Somewhere he really didn't want to be.

She and Maud should leave—but Finn's hand was still gripping hers, and Maud wasn't going anywhere. She was avidly listening.

'Because it wasn't fair,' Finn said at last. 'I

wasn't being…*magnanimous*. I had no more rights than either of you. Our father's legacy was made on a whim, and I've corrected it. I've taken legal steps now to ensure the estate's divided fairly, but right from the beginning I decided there was no need for you to know. I hate it that you have to know now.'

'But why?' Connie wailed.

'Because when Dad died you were both practically on the streets,' Finn told them, his voice softening. Becoming gentle. 'You both knew the hard way about charity. I thought…it should be yours. There was no way I had the right to own it, on nothing more than a whim of a selfish low-life. And look at what you've done with it.' He smiled at them both. He was still holding Rachel's hand, almost possessively, but his smile embraced the kids. 'Rachel, Maud, these guys are great. Connie's an up-and-coming textile designer—you should see her stuff—and Richard's almost finished his IT degree. I'm so proud of them both.'

'And we're proud of you,' Richard said gruffly. 'So when we heard you almost died…'

'We thought we'd spend some of the money

you gave us and check you for ourselves,' Connie finished for him.

'It's not money I gave you,' Finn retorted. 'That's what I don't want you to think. It's money that's rightfully yours.'

'That's nuts,' Connie said and looked at him and smiled, her eyes filling with tears again. 'You lied and we love you for it. On the plane, Richard and I talked about it. Yes, we'd have preferred that Dad left it to us, but that you came to find us… What you gave us… It was the biggest gift, that we had a father and it was his money we could use to make ourselves a life. If you'd just given it to us…'

'But we can handle it now,' Richard said gruffly. 'Because it's not the fact that we had a caring father that counts. It's that we have an awesome big brother. But no more lies,' he said, sounding suddenly stern, older than his years. 'And no more sneaking off to the ends of the earth under aliases and nearly dying and us not knowing.'

'Because we're family,' Connie declared. 'And we've found you. Now…Finn, your sister is starving. I'm buying dinner. Are you coming?

Rachel? Maud?' She beamed at all of them but Rachel tugged back from Finn and shook her head and Maud was doing the same.

'We've eaten and you have a lot to catch up on,' Rachel said. 'We're not interrupting a family reunion.'

'But the paper said that you and Rachel...' Connie's gaze was frankly hopeful and Rachel felt her colour mount.

'No,' she said.

'No?'

'No,' Finn said bluntly.

'Will you still leave tomorrow?' Maud demanded, and Finn looked even more as if he was backed up against a brick wall.

'I'm not sure.'

'Well, I guess that's better than sure,' Maud said, sounding more cheerful. 'I'm thinking black and white makes people sure. I'm thinking...you guys need to start looking at all the colours in between.'

'I told you he was a good guy,' Maud said, back in her bedroom, sounding deeply satisfied. 'So what's stopping you now?'

'Stopping me what?'

Maud sighed. 'Launching yourself straight back into his arms? Clinging like a limpet. Even proposing. Honestly, Rachel, you have a black belt in martial arts. You do what a girl has to do.'

'He can't...want me,' Rachel said in a small voice. 'I've been awful to him.'

And Maud's satisfaction turned to anger, just like that. 'Isn't that for him to decide?' she demanded. 'I think he has.'

'I've had a baby. I'm not...'

'Not what? Perfect? Don't be ridiculous. Define perfect.'

'Maud...'

'Oh, for heaven's sake, quit it with the complications.' Maud suddenly sounded weary. 'Get up tomorrow and go for it. A girl's got to do what she has to do in this life, and she has to do it for herself. All I can do is hand out handkerchiefs. And go to sleep, which you'd be well advised to do, too. If there's fighting to be done tomorrow—and there is—then you'll need all your energy.'

She looked at Rachel, seemingly deciding to

be contented with this interesting new twist life had taken. Her anger faded and she smiled.

'I just can't wait.'

Go to sleep.

Maud had issued the order but following it wasn't easy.

It was impossible.

If she was back on the *Kimberley Temptress* she might be tempted to sneak up onto the top deck and have a spa, Rachel thought. Remembering the night of the spa. Remembering Finn.

And if he left tomorrow, that was all she'd have.

Remembering Finn.

She lay awake, staring at the ceiling, listening to the sound of the distant sea.

There were lies and lies.

Ramón's lies. Finn's lies.

Black, white and grey?

Black, white and rainbow.

She thought of Connie and Richard and the lies Finn had told them, and she thought, definitely rainbow.

But…what now? Finn owned a shipping line.

She could hardly throw herself at him. Say she'd made a mistake.

Why not?

'If I had the courage...'

She stared at her bedside clock. She'd been staring at it over and over, willing the night to disappear.

Four o'clock was hardly a time to ring Reception, asking to be put through to Finn's room. They'd probably refuse. What right did she have to disturb him?

No right at all.

She lay and thought, and thought, and thought.

Five... Almost dawn. And, with that, a thought...

Low tide. She'd been watching the tides.

Dinosaurs... Footprints, only visible at low tide. The thought was suddenly front and centre.

What had Finn said? *How could I die before I see them?*

Or before I leave the country?

Maybe...

Thinking was doing her head in. What she needed was action. What she needed was to abandon her bed, slip on her shirt and shorts and head for the door.

She did.

Then she paused. Maud would sleep until breakfast but scaring Maud was not on the agenda. She'd done that once too often.

She left a note.

'Off to look for rainbows,' she wrote, and she thought Maud would know exactly what that meant. *'Back by lunchtime, rainbows or not.'*

And she thought: once I leave this note I can't come back. Not without trying.

She went.

Outside, the night was warm and still. The moon was setting over the sea, and the first blush of dawn was tinging the horizon.

The tide was so far out that the beach was half a mile wide, a vast sweep of washed sand, with the sea colourless in the pre-dawn light.

At the end of the vast beach was a rocky out-crop. A lighthouse was set on a crag overlooking a reef where dinosaurs once roamed.

He wouldn't be there.

It didn't matter. She wanted to see the dinosaur footprints anyway.

Liar.

As much a liar as Finn?

Black, white or grey?

Black, white or rainbow.

He sat on the rocky outcrop as the tide receded and watched the first pale light filter over the horizon.

There was nothing, nothing, nothing, as far as the eye could see.

He shouldn't be here. He should be back at the hotel, sleeping. He'd had to cancel his flight—Connie and Richard had been less than pleased that he'd intended to leave the day after they arrived and he'd agreed to stay on—but he knew as soon as they woke he'd be on call as tour guide.

He was their big brother.

Family.

The knowledge that they'd come half a world to reassure themselves that he was safe had touched him as he'd never been touched.

'Heading off incognito, not telling us... You could have been nothing but scattered bones on that island and where would we have been then?'

He'd told them of the legal arrangements that ensured they were financially secure even if he'd died and they'd looked at him as if he was a sandwich short of a picnic.

'We're not talking about money.'

Family.

It had crept up on him when he'd least expected it. The feeling was unbelievable but, no matter how much they were to him, he wanted more.

He wanted one battered, brave slip of a girl who held his heart in the palm of her hand.

But she didn't want it.

She couldn't trust.

'Hey. You're sitting on my rock.'

He stilled. The whole world seemed to still.

One slip of a girl was clambering up the cliff behind him. Looking exasperated.

'You'd think,' Rachel said almost conversationally, 'that if you go to the effort of waking up at five in the morning you should be able to search for dinosaur footprints without the place being overrun by tourists.'

'Tourist,' he said, and turned and smiled at her.

She smiled back. Just like that. She stood in

the pale dawn light and smiled and smiled, and something lifted deep within him.

'So it's see dinosaur footprints and die,' she said, sounding breathless. 'Or…go back to the States.'

'I'm not leaving today,' he said. 'Richard and Connie want to ride on camels.'

'So you'll watch them ride camels,' she said cautiously. 'Like you watched Maud and me.'

'That's right.'

'It still seems…lonely.'

'I'm used to lonely.'

'I'm used to mistrust,' she whispered. 'People change.'

They looked at each other. They were twenty yards apart, and yet something passed between them, so deep, so real, that no words were needed to explain it.

No words could explain it.

'Have you found the footprints?' she asked at last, her eyes not leaving his, and he shook his head.

'I was waiting for you.'

'And if I hadn't come?'

'I'd still have waited. These prints have been

here for a hundred and twenty million years. They can wait and I decided I'd wait, too, as long as it took.'

'W…wow,' she breathed. A hundred and twenty… You'd…you'd have missed breakfast. These…these footprints must be really something. You…you want to go find them?'

He rose and held out his hand. 'Yes, I do,' he said. 'If you'll come with me.'

And there was no hesitation. She stepped forward and put her hand in his, and they headed down to sea level, to the reef, to where they could see dinosaur footprints. And to whatever else lay in their future.

She became businesslike again. Rachel-the-Geologist. The prints were hard to find but Rachel seemed to know instinctively where to look. Once she found what looked to Finn to be shallow indentations in the rocks, she set about washing sand away, focusing only on what she was seeing.

He stood back and watched. And waited. This was Rachel's call, he decided. He wouldn't rush her.

Finally she stood up, wiped her sandy hands on the back of her shorts and surveyed the prints with satisfaction. Without the sand, they did look like prints. Big ones.

'They're from a decent-sized theropod,' she told him. 'I'm thinking he would have been about your height from ground to hip joint. No wonder he sank in the sandstone. These are amazing.'

They were amazing but, despite her business-like speech, he had the feeling Rachel wasn't totally zeroed in on the prints.

She was out of her comfort zone. Embarrassed?

He waited a bit longer while she examined them from all angles. While he examined her from all angles.

He could afford to wait. There was no plane to catch. Connie and Richard and Maud wouldn't be impatient. In fact, Connie and Richard and Maud would be lining up behind him right now to say: give the lady time.

Rachel stared at the prints for as long as it took to get the courage to say what she wanted to say—and then she looked up at him.

'I'm sorry,' she said at last.

'Sorry that the theropod died?'

'Well, yes,' she said, and managed a smile. 'You can't help but wonder what happened to him. I bet he wasn't shoved overboard by drug dealers.'

'Eaten by crocs?'

'There were crocs round even then, but this guy was seriously big.'

'So we might assume he lived to a ripe old age. Which was what in dinosaur terms?'

'I don't know,' she said and frowned. 'How long is a good old age for a dinosaur? I need to look it up.'

'But not today.'

'No,' she said and took a deep breath and met his gaze. 'Today's for saying sorry to you,' she said softly. 'I'm sorry I even suggested you're like Ramón. You're not the least bit like him.'

'Isn't Ramón good-looking?'

She glanced sharply at him. He smiled and she tried to smile back. The tension broke, just a bit.

'He is,' she admitted. 'He…was.'

'Well, then…'

'Okay, you're a little like Ramón,' she conceded. 'But I'm a lousy dancer.'

'You're also a lousy liar,' she said. 'You get caught out all the time.'

'I do, don't I,' he said ruefully. 'I'm sorry, too, Rachel. I messed this up from the beginning.'

'You had good intentions.'

'I'm full of them,' he said bitterly. 'They don't seem to do me any good.'

'I don't know. The baddies are behind bars.'

'There is that.'

'And I got to be castaway on a desert island, which is a story I'll be able to tell everyone in my nursing home.'

'They'll never believe you.'

'Then I want you to be there for corroboration,' she said. 'In the next door rocking chair. Nodding and saying "Too True" and "Wasn't She Brave?"'

'And telling everyone how you can make a waddy.'

'Should we tell the odd whopper about how delicious we can make roast lizard?' She chuckled, and he reached for her hands and tugged her up close. Her chuckle died.

'No more whoppers,' he said, and it was a vow.

'Black and white?'

'Just white.'

'Don't promise,' she said, suddenly urgent. 'One day you might need to tell me a lie. One day it might be kinder. Like it was kinder to tell your siblings that their father had left them money. Like it was wiser to go on the ship under an assumed name. You need to hold it in reserve. Who knows? One day it might be the only way I can be persuaded to do something. Like if the fire's licking my toes— "Jump, dear, it's not very far." I don't want you remembering your promise and saying, "Jump, dear, it's three storeys and you're bound to go splat."'

'Remind me to buy a fire extinguisher,' he said faintly. 'Rachel, we seem to be talking long-term here. Staying in high-rise hotels. Graduating to rocking chairs. Is it possible...? Could it be at all possible that you'd consider marrying me?'

She stilled. The whole world stilled.

'Finn...'

'If it's too soon, then say so,' he said urgently. 'Tell me to wait. Tell me you'll think about it. Tell me anything you like, except don't say no. A guy has to have some hope.'

'Why…why would you want to marry me?' She closed her eyes. 'Finn, I've been married.'

'You weren't married to Ramón,' he said, suddenly harsh. 'That was the biggest lie of all. A marriage is about two people loving each other. Did that…' He caught himself. 'Could…*he…*' he said the word like an expletive '…ever have loved you and treated you as he did? It's not possible, my love. It was a sham. The only good thing about your sham marriage was it produced your daughter.'

'You…you see that,' she whispered.

'My grandfather didn't go after my dad with a gun,' he told her softly, tugging her in close, 'because his existence created me. So we'll allow Ramón to continue to exist in the world, but we'll set him aside as of no importance. And not to be factored into the question I'm asking now. Which is: will you marry me? And, as for truth…as for whether what I'm saying is another sham…Rachel, I'm asking you to take me on trust—but you can trust me. I fell in love with you when you were covered in red dust, staring up at ancient wombat paintings. I fell deeper in love when I swam with you when our lives depended on it. I fell totally in love with you when I lay with you in an inch deep-puddle and felt your heartbeat against mine. I love you and I can't say truer than that. I just…love you.'

She'd pulled away a little. She was staring at a button on his shirt. It must be a really interesting button. She was staring at it as if her life depended on it.

'But you need to think about it,' he said softly. 'I understand if you need time. I have obligations. Siblings. The odd ship or eight.'

'I've met your siblings and one of your ships. They're great.'

'If Amy's based in Darwin…I could possibly base myself here,' he told her, holding her hands gently, trying hard not to pressure. 'But it does depend a bit on Connie and Richard. They're not as…solid as they seem. I might need to spend time in the States.'

And she looked up at that. A slow smile spread over her face. It was a smile he'd never seen before. It was a smile that made him…hope.

'They need you and so do I,' she said softly, but surely now, as if she'd finally accepted where her heart was leading her. 'What was it you said?

"Whither thou goest, I will go." Finn, I'm a geologist. Rocks are everywhere. If I can't teach where you are, then I'll study.' She managed a really shaky smile. 'Mind, you'll have to keep me in the manner to which I wish to become accustomed. Rock studiers don't earn much income.'

'So...' His grip on her hands tightened. So much for no pressure. 'You'd seriously consider...marrying me?'

She met his gaze full-on.

'You're an honourable scoundrel,' she whispered. 'Maud and I have decided that's the best kind.'

'I love you, Rachel.'

'Then that makes it perfect,' she said and she tugged him close. 'Because, without a word of a lie, I love you, too. I love you, my gorgeous failed undercover agent. But no more subterfuge. Just love. Will that be enough, do you think?'

'I think it will,' he said unsteadily, and he folded her into his arms and held her, feeling her heartbeat against his, knowing he was being granted a gift without price. 'I think it'll be more than enough to keep us happy for the rest of our lives. Marry me, Rachel.'

'Yes,' she said because some things were black and white. Some things were grey, some things were rainbow but not this.

This was pure, pure white.

'Yes,' she said again. 'Yes, my love, I'll marry you, with all of my heart.'

Finn stood at the base of Uluru, waiting for his bride.

They were marrying at the magnificent rock that seemed the epicentre of the entire Australian continent. The setting was a waterhole where water slipped from the massive rock face and pooled and disappeared mysteriously underground.

He'd said; 'Wherever you want in the world,' and Rachel had chosen here. Here she'd scattered her grandmother's ashes, and those of her tiny daughter. This place was her past.

Her past had held her. The ghosts of betrayal had almost destroyed her happiness, and she was facing them now, full-on. Together.

And not just with Finn, for she was surrounded.

Amy was here, playing bridesmaid, saying, 'It's not fair. I'm the eldest: I should go first,' but Amy's wedding was timed for a week later, at the magnificent Thurston homestead. Guests for this wedding could stay on for the next. It was sort of a double wedding—only they'd decreed they needed two ceremonies, for one wouldn't do either credit.

Amy was holding one small dog, bedecked in rainbow ribbons. Buster, Rachel's ancient fox terrier, had met and approved Finn by now. Finn had obviously been deemed yet another servant for one small dog, which was most satisfactory, from everyone's point of view.

Hugo was standing in as father-of-the-bride. Best man was Matty, a beefy boat-builder from Maine, who'd arrived in Broome the day after Connie and Richard, equally concerned at the press reports on what his best friend was involved in. He was still concerned—but mostly with Connie. He hadn't been able to take his eyes from her, and Maud's matchmaking abilities were being given full credit.

Maud was matron of honour. Why wouldn't she be? She beamed and beamed and beamed.

Connie had spent the last week furiously sewing. 'What theme?' she'd asked Rachel.

Rachel had simply said, 'Rainbow.'

'Excellent,' Connie said, and rainbow it was.

She'd even have put the men in rainbow if they'd agreed.

They didn't. They wore black dinner suits because, 'I want this done properly,' Finn had decreed. 'I don't want anyone saying I didn't take this wedding seriously.'

'Are you saying I shouldn't have rainbow?' Rachel had demanded and his smile had answered her all by itself.

'Rainbow's who you are,' he said softly. 'My Rachel of Rainbows.'

'And you're my honourable scoundrel. You should be in something out of Regency London. Pantaloons and top hat.'

'Heaven forbid. Unless…' He'd grown serious for a moment. 'Unless you really want it.'

'Really?' she'd teased and he looked at her and shook his head.

'I love you enough for almost anything,' he'd said slowly.

And here she was. Here it was.

The time for his marriage.

Richard had his guitar. He was playing gently in the background—something wonderful.

He was skilled, but he could play anything he liked, Finn thought. As he stood beside the waterhole and waited for his bride, he thought anything would sound wonderful right now.

Because Rachel was walking towards him. Rachel, in a wispy, floating silk gown of all the colours in the rainbow. With her hair floating free. With a bouquet of simple white frangipani. She looked stunning. She looked...

Like Rachel.

Hugo was escorting her. He was smiling and smiling—but Rachel wasn't smiling. She was looking overwhelmed, he thought, as though the enormity of what she was doing was suddenly overtaking her.

And, with a flash of insight, he thought, *She's done this before. She's taken these vows.*

The marriage celebrant was waiting, a friend of Maud's who'd flown from Darwin. She was beaming.

Everyone was beaming but the bride.

In a moment it'd start. Rachel would be asked

to make the vows she'd made before, and suddenly Finn knew why she was hesitating. Memories were superimposing themselves—memories that had no place to be here.

It wasn't this place. The memories here were good. It was the service itself, the words…

Words she'd tried to mean before.

This time was different.

He had to make it different.

Instinctively he stepped forward and took her hand, and then turned so they were facing the small group of people they knew and loved. He pressed her hand, and then he spoke.

'In a moment Dorothy will ask us to make some vows,' he said, partly to their friends, but mostly talking to Rachel. He was talking to the woman he loved. 'We've decided we'll take those vows, and we will mean them. But, before we do…I have one of my own to add.'

He tugged Rachel towards him, he met her questioning gaze and he smiled at her.

'I ask all here to witness,' he said slowly, seriously, 'that if I ever knowingly hurt this woman who I love with all my heart, then I give full and open permission for Hugo to transfer me to one barren Kimberley island with nothing but one rain jacket and one waddy. And I'll sign a document to swear it, this very day.'

There was a ripple of laughter. The tension faded from Rachel's face and he saw the first trace of a smile.

'I swear,' he repeated. 'My love, I swear it. I will never hurt you.'

'My honourable scoundrel,' she whispered. 'Oh, Finn, of course you won't hurt me.'

'And you?' he asked. 'Is there anything you'd like to say before we ask Dorothy to do her bit?'

'I'd ask to come with you,' she said softly. 'On any island you're ever left on. Because, left alone, I doubt you could even handle a waddy. Or put up flags. So maybe we should just agree not to hurt.'

'I'm cool with that,' he said. 'So I believe it's a bargain, made before witnesses. And now I need to ask you…Rachel Cotton, do you trust me enough to want Dorothy to marry us?'

'I'm happy to carry on,' Dorothy said mildly. 'When you're ready.'

And Rachel looked directly into his face and what she saw there made her smile. It wasn't laughter, though. It was something far, far deeper, and it was something that promised to last a lifetime.

Her smile widened. She smiled and she smiled, as a bride should on her wedding day.

'I'm ready,' she whispered as the shadows disappeared to nothing. Only joy remained. 'I'm ready for whatever life throws at us. I'm ready for rainbows, Finn Kinnard; for anything as long as we're together.'

* * * * *

Mills & Boon® Large Print
May 2013

BEHOLDEN TO THE THRONE
Carol Marinelli

THE PETRELLI HEIR
Kim Lawrence

HER LITTLE WHITE LIE
Maisey Yates

HER SHAMEFUL SECRET
Susanna Carr

THE INCORRIGIBLE PLAYBOY
Emma Darcy

NO LONGER FORBIDDEN?
Dani Collins

THE ENIGMATIC GREEK
Catherine George

THE HEIR'S PROPOSAL
Raye Morgan

THE SOLDIER'S SWEETHEART
Soraya Lane

THE BILLIONAIRE'S FAIR LADY
Barbara Wallace

A BRIDE FOR THE MAVERICK MILLIONAIRE
Marion Lennox